THE **DREAMSEEKER** TRILOGY
SILVER CLOUD

THE **DREAMSEEKER** TRILOGY

SILVER CLOUD

Jenny Oldfield

Illustrated by Paul Fisher Johnson

h
*Hodder
Children's
Books*

A division of Hodder Headline Limited

For Kate and Eve, as they seek their dreams.

First published in Great Britain in 2002
by Hodder Children's Books

A Catalogue record for this book is available
from the British Library

ISBN 0 340 85108 2

Typeset by Avon Dataset Ltd, Bidford-on-Avon, Warks

Printed and bound in Great Britain by
The Guernsey Press Co. Ltd, Channel Isles

Hodder Children's Books
a division of Hodder Headline Ltd
338 Euston Road
London NW1 3BH

As flies to wanton boys, are we to the gods;
They kill us for their sport.

King Lear, IV i. 44–5

WHITE WATER SIOUX FAMILY TREE

Red Hawk m. **White Deer**

(Chief of White Water Sioux)

Unnamed m. **River That Flies Tribeswoman**

(Red Hawk's brother)   (MiniConjou)

Swift Elk m. **Shining Star**

(Died at Thunder Ridge)

Black Kettle m. **Unnamed**

(Died at Thunder Ridge)

Four Winds

Hidden Moon

GOOD SPIRITS	EVIL SPIRITS
Wakanda	**Anteep**
(Maker of All Good Things)	(Source of All Evil)
|	∫
Ghost Horse	**Unktehi**
(A major animal spirit)	(Guardian of Yellow Water)
∫	|
Silver Cloud	**Yietso**
(Spirit messenger)	(Shape-shifting servant)

PART 1: THE DREAM

ONE

The old man sat by the dying fire. He wore a blanket around his hunched shoulders and stared into the embers.

The boy, Four Winds, watched and listened sadly.

'I am very old. My sun is set,' his grandfather began. 'Once I was a warrior. *Iki 'cize waon 'kon.* Now it is over.'

A burned-out log shifted, releasing red sparks into the night sky. Four Winds followed their whirling, fading dance, then looked back at the old man.

True, it was a lined face. The skin was criss-crossed

3

with years of struggle. The hands were gnarled like the roots of a tree.

'Soon I will lie down to rise no more.'

Four Winds leaned forward to stir the embers. He concentrated on the pattern of the sparks in the sky.

'Listen, my son. Once I was a warrior. I fought my enemies and feasted my friends. My people were around me like the sands of the shore. They have passed away, they have died like the grass in winter, they have gone to the mountains. *Hena 'la yelo.* It is over.'

Standing abruptly, Four Winds made as if to cast another log on the fire. He didn't want to hear this lamenting. He preferred the tales of his grandfather's youth, of his beaded war shirt hung with ermine pelts, of the eagle feathers that adorned his headdress. Red Hawk the warrior, Chief of the White Water band of the great Sioux tribe.

'I will speak,' Red Hawk insisted, his face lit up by a fountain of fresh sparks. 'When I look back now from this high hill of my old age, I see a time of plenty. There was food for our stomachs then, and we heard no man's commands.'

'That time will come again,' Four Winds said softly.

The sparks faded and left the old man's face in

darkness. 'You are young,' he said. 'The only son of my only son.'

Here was more pain and sadness. The boy turned away from the fire. The face of his dead father came back to him in the moving shadows, his eyes dark and gentle. His mother too was there in the cold night, watching over him.

Red Hawk gazed at his grandson. 'Much has ended,' he insisted. 'The Comanches came on horseback from the south. They seized the land of White Water that the Great Spirit gave us. Our people died in the mud, our women were sold into slavery.'

Four Winds closed his eyes to block out the picture of his father, Swift Elk, slain on the battlefield. Of his beautiful mother, Shining Star, snatched away in the dead of night.

'Now winter comes and the White Water people have no home. The Wild Dog Comanches take the fish from our rivers and the buffalo from our plains. We must leave our homeland on a trail of tears and walk to our deaths in the frozen mountains to the west. *Hena 'la yelo*. It is over.'

Four Winds left his grandfather at last. He respected the years that the old man had lived and the suffering he had gone through, but his boy's heart wouldn't accept defeat.

He walked between the tipis towards the river and the great plain beyond. A million stars shone in the sky. Under the moonlight, the sea of pale grass rippled in the wind.

Why must they depart because the Comanches ordered it? It was a shameful thing to leave the homeland, cast out like dogs. And Four Winds was sure that the Great Spirit didn't wish it.

'We must stay and fight!' he said to the night sky.

You are a boy. His mother's voice whispered to him from the blackness. *You cannot fight.*

Thirteen summers have passed since you gave me life, he muttered. *I call that old enough to carry a war club!*

Against men on swift horses while you have only your own poor speed and your boy's strength of arm?

'Mother!' he whispered, angered by the reminder of the Comanche band's unfair advantage.

Two summers back, the Wild Dogs under Snake Eye had ridden their strange, deer-like beasts into the Sioux village. The creatures had carried them to swift victory over the White Water band. Swift Elk had been among the dead, pierced through the heart by a Comanche lance. Shining Star and many other Sioux women had vanished from their tipis.

Since then, the small band of survivors had taken refuge on rocky heights, driven further from the buffalo and the fish. They had grown hungry, lost more men in Comanche raids, until now only five warriors remained out of fifty, plus the medicine man, Matotope. Three boys of similar age to Four Winds longed to fight alongside their elders, but Four Winds' own grandmother, White Deer, stood between them and their wish.

'A boy must go out to Spider Rock before he can fight,' she insisted. 'He must fast and seek the powers of the Great One through a vision in that sacred place. Until then he lacks the wisdom for battle and must stay by the tipi.'

Four Winds felt angered by his grandmother's words – yet he knew it was the way of the tribe.

And now his grandfather said it was over. They must roll up their tents, strap them on the travois and have the dogs drag them high into the mountains to escape Snake Eye. But escape into what?

'We will all die,' he told the stars. He was touched by the gloom of his grandfather. It fell over him like a heavy blanket which would not let him breathe.

* * *

'How soon must we move on?' Four Winds asked his grandmother, White Deer.

It was early next morning, and the old woman had risen and was busy skinning and treating the hide of an antelope. She worked with a sharp bone tool, staking the skin on to a wooden frame then scraping it clean.

'That depends,' White Deer told him, scooping water from a wooden bowl and washing down the skin. Then she scraped some more.

'On what?' Four Winds was impatient. He'd spent a night in the tipi, rolled in his blanket, unable to sleep. He knew that his grandmother would pretend that this was just one more move, from summer camp to winter quarters. But his talk with Red Hawk had convinced him that this wasn't so. This time, it was the Comanches driving them out once and for all.

'On my husband, your grandfather,' she replied evenly, scooping and scraping. The skin, once it had been rubbed down with boiled brain, liver and fat, would be used to repair an old tipi.

'And how will he decide?'

The old woman sighed and looked up. 'Four Winds, my little Kola, who can answer that question?'

'*Kola*' had been his mother's nickname for him. It meant 'friend'. Now the sound of it ran through him like the cold autumn wind.

'Kola,' White Deer said again. 'Come, fetch me more water, or this skin will never soften.'

So he went and brought water from a creek which ran down to meet the white water below. He held the bowl under a small waterfall and let it fill to the brim. When he looked up again, he was startled by what he saw.

The bowl dropped to the ground. For a moment he thought that Snake Eye and his people had appeared on the rocky horizon, that the Comanches had found the Sioux band's latest hideout and had come to drive them higher, above the snowline into the white wilderness.

But then he made out the shapes in the morning mist more clearly. It was the creatures that the enemy called by the name of horse – those beasts that seemed like a mixture of elk and deer, but were hornless and could be ridden by a man.

Four Winds breathed more easily. For now there seemed to be no Comanches nearby – only the creatures with long necks, and hair falling gracefully to one side. They stood still and silent in the mist, looking down on him, eleven or twelve of them lining the horizon.

He stooped to pick up the bowl and refill it. The cold water ran over his wrists, the creek splashed over the rocks. Did the appearance of the horses mean that the Wild Dogs were nearby, he wondered. Perhaps he should hurry back to the tipis to warn his grandfather.

Another glance at the horizon told Four Winds that the creatures were about to depart. Some had already turned and were melting into the mist. Others stamped their hooves and made a strange snorting noise. Only one stood in the same place as before, letting the wind tug at his mane, his eyes fixed on the boy by the waterfall.

Four Winds felt the power of the horse's gaze. Not a single muscle moved as he communicated his presence across a gap of a hundred paces. He was silvery grey with a pure white mane and tail. Strange but beautiful, Four Winds thought. He had often heard of wonderful happenings from the earliest times, of creatures that came from the sun or else out of the earth. He had learned not to do anything harmful, but to be still and wait. Surely the silver horse was part of the Great Spirit's work, and He was present in him, as He was in all four-legged creatures, and the winged birds and the mountains, the rivers, the grasses, the trees.

The boy understood this and was no longer afraid.

He smiled at the pale horse in the morning mist, then turned and took the bowl of water to White Deer.

'What do you know of the Comanche horse?' Red Hawk asked Matotope.

'The creature runs swift as the elk. It has the grace of the antelope,' the medicine man replied. He'd answered the call to the chief's tipi in his own time, first dressing in his ceremonial robe of eagle feathers, then singing praises to the sacred creatures of the sky.

'I don't need your wisdom to know this,' Red Hawk replied. 'This much I have seen with my own eyes. What else?'

Matotope ignored the interruption. 'He has the strength of a young buffalo and the courage of a mountain lion.'

'This is so. And he bears the enemy of our People on his back,' the old man pointed out. The cold had made his chest heave and rattle and his hands tremble. 'He makes the Comanche all-powerful. Surely he is an evil spirit, to permit the destruction of our White Water sons.'

The medicine man bowed his head and remained silent.

'Well?' Red Hawk spoke sharply. Time was running

out, night was darkening around him.

'I have been to Spider Rock and talked with the four sacred animals,' Matotope said. The medicine man was in his prime, smooth-skinned beneath his feathered robe. About his body he wore a buckskin pouch filled with animal bones, shells and beads.

'You asked them in turn about this creature?'

Matotope nodded. 'I spoke with the Mountain Lion who guards the north and the Bear of the west. They knew nothing of this being. Neither did Wolf, guardian of the east.'

'But the Snake of the south?' Red Hawk prompted.

'Snake listened and told me everything. Our brothers the Ute, the Kiowa, the Apache and the Caddo already know of the horse. Our enemies the Comanche travelled south into the desert land and found people from beyond the sea. They were full of wonder at the creatures they saw there and brought many back to the plains.'

'To use as weapons of war against us,' the old man said bitterly. 'For two years Sioux blood has been spilt on the battlefield because of the horse. I have lost my only son. What advice did Snake give about *that?*'

'I asked for none,' the shaman said. 'It is as it is, and I have told you all I heard.'

For a while the two men sat in silence.

'When I turn to the east, I see no dawn,' Red Hawk said at last. 'What are my People to do, where are they to go in the coming generations?'

'It will be as the Great Spirit wills,' Matotope murmured, uneasy because he had reached the limits of his wisdom. The bones and beads in his medicine bag couldn't bring back the dead warriors or stop the Wild Dog braves.

'What is this horse? Is he a messenger like the owl or a guard of the Great Spirit? Does he advise the gods, or is he a mere servant like the dog?'

With a proud look, the shaman dismissed the old chief's questions. 'Better not to waste time wondering. Better to tell your People to roll up their tipis and move on before the snow comes,' he advised. 'The grass is dying and the leaves are brown. Soon Snake Eye will be here.'

'We have some time – a little.' Friendly scouts had told Red Hawk that the Comanches had put up their lodges in the east, ten days' walk away. The enemy didn't show any sign of wanting to pursue them at present. 'If we move from here, know that we move to our certain deaths, away from our homeland, in the white mountains.'

13

Slowly Matotope nodded. This was so.

'No.' Red Hawk's voice gained strength as he made his decision. 'You, Matotope, must go again to Spider Rock.'

The medicine man's eyes narrowed and glittered.

'Stay two suns and one moon. Fast and pray. Call upon the spirit of this mysterious creature, the Horse. Ask him to guide us away from danger.'

Matotope stood. The feathers on his cloak fluttered as he moved.

'Tell the Ghost Horse that he is our only hope,' the old man insisted. 'The People need food and warmth for the winter, and the strength to fight the Comanches who use the horse with ill will against us.'

'I will do this,' Matotope promised.

'Without the help of the Ghost Horse, the tribe will vanish. I am old. A People's dream has died on the battleground. It was a beautiful dream. But the nation's hoop is broken, there is no centre.'

The medicine man nodded gravely. 'In two suns and one moon I shall return.'

Red Hawk's eyes were filled with tears. '*Maka akanl wicasa iyuha el,*' he said. Go in peace.

TWO

White Deer left off
scraping the antelope skin
and looked up at the
sky. Trouble had taken root
deep in her heart and
would not go away.

Yes, it was as Red Hawk
said, time and again: the
hoop was broken. The
dream was lost.

Her son's son appeared
on the hill, carrying
water. His youth pained
her. A boy approaching
manhood, with the slight
shoulders and slender
waist of a child, Kola's
legs were growing long
like his father's, his black
hair thick like his

15

mother's. Her heart ached for him.

'I saw horses,' he told her.

White Deer scooped water from the bowl and trickled it over the animal skin. 'How many?'

Four Winds showed her with his fingers. 'One was beautiful. He was grey like the mist, silver like the water under moonlight.'

She frowned. Taking the bone tool, she scraped the remaining blood and flesh from the hide. 'I know nothing of horses. Only that they bear our enemies.'

'There were no Wild Dogs with the herd I saw on the hill,' the boy assured his grandmother. 'These horses belonged to no man. They were free like the elk and the buffalo.'

The old woman grunted. This water was cold, the skin stubborn. She worked flesh out of the corners then laid the side of her knife against a rock to sharpen the edge. 'When I have finished with the hide I want you to help me cut the meat from this animal into strips. We must hang it in the sun.'

Four Winds frowned over the woman's work. White Deer must be angry with him for his talk about the horses. Yet she hadn't seen them. 'They stood and watched me at the waterfall,' he insisted. 'I wasn't afraid.'

16

'You are young.'

This was what she always said. Meaning, your judgement is shallow, there is no wisdom inside a head that bears no grey hairs.

White Deer glanced up at Four Winds' guarded face. 'You say this animal is beautiful. But a flower may be beautiful and kill with its poison. And listen, before you defend this creature called the horse. Remember that under the skin of an animal beats a heart like a human heart.'

The boy nodded. As a child hardly able to walk, he had been taught this by his mother. That animals do not look like people, but they think like people do, and they really *are* people under their pelts.

'The heart of the buffalo is good,' his grandmother continued. 'He came from under the earth and swam a great river. He brings us life. But the coyote bears a trickster's heart. He is cunning and greedy, sent here by Anteep, the wicked chief of the lower world.'

'The horse is not sent by Anteep,' Four Winds said stubbornly.

White Deer sighed. 'Wait and see,' was all she said.

Matotope opened the flap of Red Hawk's tipi, stooped low and went out into the morning air.

There was a rattle in the old man's chest and a slowness in his brain. Always his thoughts flew back instead of forward. He came up with solutions that led nowhere.

The shaman took a deep breath and looked around the village. There were only ten tipis now, hurriedly thrown up and clinging to a steep, treeless mountainside. Three of the tipis contained only old women and children. Five were still painted with warriors' marks to celebrate victories in battle. The ninth belonged to Red Hawk and White Deer, the tenth to Matotope himself.

Once there had been eighty lodges in the village. Smoke had risen through every smoke hole; the hearths were places of comfort and plenty. Beyond their rows of tents had stretched a green plain teeming with buffalo, elk and antelope.

Matotope's eye rested on the figure of White Deer stooped over a wooden frame, washing and softening a single antelope hide. The meat from this one animal was all the White Water band had in store for the winter ahead.

And what had the old chief told him? Go once more to the sacred rock. Call upon the spirit of the Horse to save us!

Red Hawk had a rattle in his chest and his eyes set on death. A younger chief would have listened to advice and done what the Kiowa and Apache had done in the desert lands to the south. Fight fire with fire, they said. If the Comanches have the Horse, then so must the Apache, for how can a man on foot fight a fair battle with a man on a horse?

Two summers ago, the fathers of the Sioux Nation had gathered at Thunder Ridge. Tall Bull, Red Feather, Lone Wolf and Spotted Tail had come together with Red Hawk and heard of the White Waters' troubles. Twenty of their braves had already died at the hand of the swift Comanche enemy.

The old men smoked pipes and made empty promises. They would not hear of carrying out raids to steal this mysterious creature, the Horse, from their enemies. Wakanda, the Great Spirit, does not wish it, they said.

Matotope smiled bitterly at the memory as he slid his feather cloak from his back and strode towards his tipi. Fight fire with fire. Set horse against horse. That had been his advice. But Red Hawk set his face against it and his People had died.

So let it be.

* * *

'Matotope is to go to the sacred place,' the children whispered.

'I saw him painting his body inside his tipi,' one said. 'He put on his bonnet of eagle feathers and fastened his medicine bundle to his wampum belt.'

'Then he is going to Spider Rock,' they said in awed voices.

Four Winds listened to their chatter inside the tents of the grandmothers. Outside, a wind blew down from the mountain tops, so the women had hung the dew cloth around the walls of the tipi to keep out the cold. 'When does Matotope journey to the rock?' he asked Hidden Moon, the girl who gave most of the facts.

'Tonight,' she told him. 'When the stars are clear in the sky, with the full moon to guide him.'

'Chief Red Hawk is very sick,' a small child said. 'They say he may not see another sun rise in the east.'

'Hush!' Hidden Moon warned. 'Wakanda will be angry with you for saying so.'

The boy drew a deep breath then fell silent. He crept on to the knees of one of the old women and hid against her striped woollen shawl.

Hidden Moon saw Four Winds rise and leave the tent, his head hanging low. Quickly she followed him. 'Is your grandfather really so ill?' she asked him.

Four Winds nodded. 'He carries a deep hurt. He suffers for the People.'

'He has done all he can to save us.' Hidden Moon was the grandchild of Red Hawk's brother who had married into the River That Flies band belonging to the Miniconjou tribe. Her father had died in battle beside Four Winds' father, Swift Elk. The boy and girl were tied by blood.

Four Winds was grateful for the kind words. He walked with his cousin through the camp, past the closed flap of his grandfather's tent. 'Red Hawk remembers the wonder of the wide open plain,' he explained. 'Now all that is overthrown. His last hope lies with Matotope and the spirits of Spider Rock.'

'I don't trust Matotope,' Hidden Moon said simply.

Four Winds looked sharply into her dark brown eyes. Then he decided to make a joke of it. 'Hush, Wakanda will be angry!'

'I don't care,' the girl said, still serious. 'I say that Matotope's medicine is not strong, to let our People die like dogs in the mud. His advice led my father and your father to their deaths at Burning Rock. Thirty men on foot against a hundred on horseback, and Matotope in his holy wisdom told your grandfather they must stand and fight!'

The boy took his cousin by the arm and led her up the hill to the place where he had seen the horses. 'This is dangerous talk,' he warned. 'Don't let the others hear you.'

'I don't care!' With the wind tugging at her braided hair and the fringe of her buckskin skirt, Hidden Moon defied him. 'If I was a man I would fight in the name of Black Kettle, my father. I would steal at night into the camp of the Wild Dogs and kill as many Comanches as I could!'

Four Winds was amused. He laughed in the girl's face.

'Laugh then!' she scorned. 'One day you will be a man and you will fight in the name of Swift Elk, your father. Imagine how it feels to be a girl, left by the hearth with your grandmother, waiting night after night for the enemy to raid your empty camp and sell you into slavery!'

'That's how it is with me now,' he admitted. 'Left at home with the old women and children.'

Hidden Moon saw that her angry words had hit home. 'But you will be a man one day,' she insisted more gently. 'And, if it is not too late, you will be a warrior.'

* * *

Matotope was leaving at sunset, so Four Winds must hurry. His cousin's words had disturbed him deeply and made him feel ashamed.

Why did he, a boy with thirteen summers behind him, sit at home with the old women? His spear arm was growing strong. He had trained his eye to see a target and his hand to aim true. Why accept defeat without a struggle?

Quickly he made his way down from the waterfall to his grandfather's tipi. He was about to raise the flap and enter, when his grandmother stepped out.

'Red Hawk is sleeping,' she said quietly.

'I need to talk with him,' Four Winds tried to explain.

'Later.' White Deer laid a hand on his wrist.

There would be no later, the boy knew now. This would be his only chance. If his grandfather was asleep then he must plead with his grandmother. 'I wish to go with Matotope to the sacred rock,' he said.

White Deer shook her head as if an insect had landed on her cheek. 'I must fetch logs for Red Hawk's fire,' she said, hurriedly moving away.

'I mean it, grandmother. I want to go on a dream quest.'

23

'You are too young.' The old woman went for her logs to the stack which Four Winds had chopped. They were out of hearing of the rest of the band, in a windy place overlooking a deep canyon.

'I want to go,' he insisted.

She lifted two logs and thrust them into his arms. 'Young and foolish,' she lamented. 'Speak no more.'

He obeyed, knowing her well. Soon she herself would break the silence.

'A seeker of dreams walks away from his childhood, he says goodbye to childish things,' she said in a sad, low voice. Her thin hands trembled as she lifted the next log. 'He can never be simple again.'

'It is time,' he insisted. 'My father told me that he walked out to seek the spirits in the fourteenth summer of his life. I have thirteen summers. What is the difference?'

'You leave behind the boy, Kola. You must become the man, Four Winds.' His grandmother shook her head and let her sorrow show. 'It is I who have nursed you, my child, I who have taught you to sing and play. How can I lose the boy that I love?'

'And how can I remain the boy when the man's voice calls?' he pleaded. 'Tonight Matotope will follow the North Star to Spider Rock. I must go with him to fast, and call on the spirits to give me the power to fight.'

'That is not a man's voice, it is the voice of foolishness!' she said as she struggled to pile more logs into his arms.

Four Winds staggered under the weight. 'I must purify my body and go to the spirits, fast and pray for a visitation,' he said stubbornly. 'Or else I will fight the Comanches without the protection of Wakanda. For I will not stay in the tipi like a coward when my arm is strong!'

'Kola!' White Deer sighed with tears in her eyes. She made him put the logs down on the ground and sit cross-legged with her in the cold wind. Then she took out a small pouch made of lizard skin from the folds of her skirt. 'I found this on the tipi floor on the night your mother, Shining Star, was taken by the Comanches.'

'What is it?' Four Winds asked. His grandmother's tears had made him sad.

'Inside is the sacred cord from her body which was severed at your birth. Shining Star kept it safe in this pouch, knowing that Lizard promises long life. Her last thought when she was taken was for you and your future. It was a message to me to guard you and keep you safe.'

He watched his grandmother turn the small leather pouch in her crooked fingers. 'Thank you,' he murmured. 'This gives me strength.'

'My heart is breaking,' she moaned. 'My husband turns towards death and my son's son takes his leave.'

'But grandmother, your teaching has always been that we must look and listen for the good of the whole People. I learned this at your knee.'

She nodded. ' "In all of your actions cast away your self," ' she quoted. ' "Have always in view not only the present, but also the coming generations." It is true, according to the Great Law.'

'And all things are the work of the Great Spirit,' he reminded her.

' "He is within all things, the trees, the grasses, the rivers, the mountains, the four-legged animals and the winged creatures," ' she chanted, her voice halting, and sighing all the while. ' "We should understand this deeply and in our hearts, then we will fear and love and know the Great Spirit, and we will be and act and live as He intends." '

Once more Four Winds let the silence flow.

'Come,' White Deer said at last. 'We will prepare a

bath of sweetgrass. When Red Hawk awakes I will tell him that his only grandson, Four Winds, is setting out on his dream quest!'

THREE

The old man slept on.

Perhaps it was his last sleep of all. Knowing this, the mood in the village was heavy. Amongst the wind battered tipis, the women went quietly about their work and the men huddled round fires, waiting.

Four Winds watched White Deer talking with Matotope. He had bathed in the sweetgrass water and taken his last food before he set off to seek his dream. With a stomach full of antelope meat and berries, he was ready to begin.

But he could see the medicine man arguing

29

with his grandmother, and so he went closer to the fire.

'Only Red Hawk can say yes or no to a dream quest,' Matotope pointed out. On the ground in front of him lay a small blanket, and on this were arranged beads, bones, herbs and a bird's head – the precious contents of the shaman's medicine bundle. 'Until Red Hawk wakes, the boy must stay here in the village.'

'But you can take him with you to Spider Rock,' White Deer pointed out. 'My husband would wish that his son's son should seek out the vision that will make him a man.'

'Four Winds is too young,' Matotope said. Noting the boy's approach, he voiced his doubts openly. 'My own quest is a hard one and the future of the White Water band relies on it. Why should I take along a child to worry over?'

'I will take care of myself,' Four Winds said. 'No one need trouble themselves about me!'

White Deer smiled faintly. Age had taught her to accept the boastfulness of youth without comment. To be young meant to be strong and proud, bold in front of the wolf, fast as the running deer. She remembered.

'I have purified myself and eaten. I am ready,' Four Winds insisted.

Matotope shrugged. He placed the line of objects inside his painted leather pouch. 'Make your farewells,' he grunted. 'When the North Star appears in the sky, we begin.'

'So, you are going to Spider Rock.' Hidden Moon stood outside the children's tipi. Behind her, the sun set fiery red in the west.

Inside the tent, the younger ones whispered together about their friend Kola's vision quest.

'Because of the challenge you threw in my face,' Four Winds confessed.

The girl nodded gravely. 'Then, Kola, you will fight in the name of your father, Swift Elk, and you will remember my father, Black Kettle, who died at his side.'

'I will,' he promised.

Hidden Moon smiled, turned and stooped to enter the tipi.

Then, with dusk settling on the hillside and the swallows whirling and swooping overhead, Four Winds went to each of the five warriors left in the White Water band.

First Sun Dancer clasped the boy by the arm and wished him well. He reminded him of his Sioux fathers who had fought before him in generations past.

Running Fox and Little Thunder each spoke of the White Water homeland and told Four Winds to put his trust in Wakanda, the Great Spirit, He who made all things.

Outside One Horn's tent, the boy promised to open himself through fasting to the visit from the Maker of All. One Horn was the oldest of the warriors. He bore the scars of battle across his chest and arm. There was a sad look in his eye as he clasped Four Winds' hand. 'Tonight, when you are gone, we will hold a ceremony, the *Alo'wanpi*. We will sing to the spirit called White Buffalo Maiden so that only good will befall you.'

Finally the boy went to visit Three Bears in his tipi. Smoke spiralled up through the smoke hole. A war bonnet of eagle feathers hung from the wall.

'Seek in the sacred place for the wisdom to defeat the enemy,' Three Bears advised. 'Open your heart to the messengers. Come back strong and ready to fight.'

Once more, Four Winds promised. For the first time, as he stepped out into the gathering darkness to meet with Matotope, his insides fluttered as though there were birds inside the cage of his ribs, flapping to escape.

He saw his grandmother waiting quietly outside her tipi, old and thin, white-haired. She held her hands

clasped in front of her and made no move towards
him.

You will never be simple again.

He gazed at her across the ashes and blackened logs
of yesterday's fire, then he held up the lizard pouch.

White Deer bowed her head.

Then Matotope came and pointed to the first star in
the night sky. He was stripped to the waist, dressed
only in buckskin trousers and moccasins, with green
beads and three black feathers in his hair.

The birds inside Four Winds' ribcage fought to be
free. He took a deep breath. The North Star, shining
like his mother in the sky, called him.

Matotope and the boy walked in silence through the
night.

They came down from the cold mountain into the
warm valley of their ancestors, travelling by the water's
edge through willow thickets where Coyote made a
midnight meal of bobcat and Otter dammed his creek
and watched for the glint of fish in the water.

As the sun rose and the birds of the air began to
sing, Four Winds followed Matotope through a deep
canyon where the water ran white over boulders,
between black cliffs. He felt the spray on his bare skin.

Suddenly he lost his footing on the wet rocks, fell, and felt the foaming stream grab hold of him. He swirled downstream, dragged under by the current. But he kicked hard, swam against the flow. With a sudden effort he lunged at an overhanging branch, caught hold of it and dragged himself clear.

Twenty paces ahead of him, Matotope didn't even glance over his shoulder.

Four Winds smiled grimly and reminded himself to include an otter's paw in his own medicine bundle when the time came to make one. He would need the animal's strength underwater if he were to survive in the white water rapids of his homeland.

Soon though, they left the bank of the winding river and cut off towards the east, climbing at first to a rocky ridge, then standing to catch their breath.

The boy felt the warmth of the sun. It shone low across the new land that faced them, casting long shadows amongst the cedar trees. He saw no sign of the sacred Spider Rock on the far horizon, but held his silence. Matotope wouldn't welcome childish questions.

The morning grew hot. The breeze that had stirred the leaves of the cottonwoods dropped away. They were through the stand of trees, treading softly towards a low, flat horizon, feeling the sun's rays beat down on their backs.

As they made for the summit of the hill, Four Winds' legs began to grow weary and sweat trickled down the nape of his neck. Yet Matotope never broke his long stride. In fact, he chose the gruelling climb to begin to talk to the boy.

'You completed *inipi* before you came?' he checked.

Four Winds recalled his sweetgrass sweat bath and nodded.

'It is where the earth, the air, fire and water join together to cleanse your spirit.'

'I know.' The boy resented the shaman's reminder.

'And you come to the sacred site with humility?' Matotope asked, with one eyebrow raised in his high, broad forehead.

Four Winds was silent. He realised that he was proud in his heart.

'Well, the days on Spider Rock may bring you to a proper sense of your true place among the White Water Sioux. And remember, many boys seek a vision and many fail to find one. They must come again and again, endure many fasts before the Great Spirit appears.'

In spite of his weariness, Four Winds picked up speed. He walked ahead of the shaman. There was no time for him to fail and come again. The Comanches would soon roll up their summer tipis and come with their horses towards Red Hawk's hideout. It might only be a matter of days before his People were driven into the snowy wastes. 'I will open my heart and meet with Wakanda,' he insisted. 'I will be ready.'

Matotope cut off on to a new track. 'Good words,' he said. 'But good words do not last long before they must amount to something. Words do not pay for your dead father. They do not protect his grave.'

Driven into silence, Four Winds followed again. He trod in the shaman's dusty footsteps, cresting the next ridge and looking down on an exposed plain of red sand. Far off, flat layers of red sandstone rose to meet the sky and amongst them stood two tall needles of rock which drew the boy's gaze.

'Spider Rock and Talking Gods Rock,' Matotope told him. 'The spirit, Spider, lives on the highest peak.'

The flutters inside Four Winds' chest started up once more. 'Why is the tip of her rock coloured white?' he wanted to know.

'Those are the bones of children she has captured and devoured. The Talking Gods keep watch and tell her who must be taken prisoner. There is no escape from Spider's web.'

Four Winds knew that it was the craft and skill of the Spider which made her so powerful. It was from underneath her rock that the spirits might be expected to answer a human call. Still, he felt a strong fear of approaching the place.

For the first time the boy was glad of Matotope's wisdom. As they descended on to the plain and trudged through the wasteland of stone and sand, he put questions about the animal spirits whose help they were seeking.

'When I call to Wakanda in the great sky above, which name shall I pray for?'

'I can't tell you. You must judge what is best.'

'How can I judge without guidance?' Four Winds needed more knowledge than he'd gained from stories at his mother and grandmother's knees.

'Very well. Each creature possesses a quality that a warrior might desire,' Matotope explained. 'When I made my dream quest many summers ago I called upon the Hawk because he is the surest bird of prey. Others call for the Deer because she can endure thirst in the desert. Or for the watchfulness of the Frog, or for the Crow who is swift and direct in flight.'

'Then I might call for the Eagle?' Four Winds asked. 'For he flies highest of all and sees all things.'

But the medicine man shook his head. 'Only the boldest may call upon the Eagle. The Master of Life, the Great Spirit, has warned that although all creatures gain power from the Sun, the Eagle is set above the rest. His help often brings added danger.'

'Then perhaps I will ask Wakanda who my best messenger would be,' Four Winds decided.

Matotope shrugged and said Four Winds must do as he chose. Meanwhile, they walked across the hot plain.

At midday the shaman took his place. He raised his outstretched palm to the sun and began his chant. ' "*Tate ou ye topa kin*". The four winds are blowing. In a sacred manner I call to them!'

Four Winds watched the solitary figure under the tall column of red rock. He examined the circles of white stones placed at its base and recognised them as medicine wheels. The pattern of stones protected the traveller and guided him in his quest.

It was time to begin. Turning his back on Spider Rock, he examined Talking Gods Rock.

The tower was shorter and thicker, with a ledge at its base which faced west. Four Winds chose the ledge for his own search. Far away, through a shimmering haze, he made out a line of blue mountains.

He climbed up to the ledge, threw back his shoulders and reached out his hand to the blue sky.

> ' "*Wakan yan*
> *mica kelo*
> *nagi ksa pawan*
> *maka hewaye*
> *wakan yan*
> *mica kelo*
> *kola*
> *wanma yanka yo.*" '

Four Winds described how the Great One made a wise spirit especially for him. How he, Four Winds, had come to a sacred place, and behold, he had come in search of the spirit.

Then he waited. He waited without food or water, as the sun sank low in the sky. 'I am patient,' he told the Maker of All Things. 'I will be here when the sun sets and the stars appear. I will remain through the cold night and call again at the dawning of the day!'

Chanting and praying, the boy remained strong.

On the second day, at the foot of Spider Rock, Matotope continued to ask the questions that the old chief had sent him to deliver. '*Wakan tanka*, oh Great One, I call upon the spirit of this mysterious creature, the Horse. I ask him to guide us, the White Water People, out of danger!'

The shaman was stiff and weary. Once before he had come to this rock and talked with the four sacred animals. He had learned little and feared that his powers were fading. His return had taught him that this was indeed so.

But Matotope would die before he would go back to his People and admit his failure.

Maybe it was because his heart was no longer pure. There had been other times when he'd spoken good words and committed bad acts. And once, in battle, he'd betrayed the Sioux custom of the *Cante Tinz*, the Strong Hearts. Fighting beside Black Kettle and Swift Elk at Burning Ridge, in his medicine man's helmet of buffalo horns and eagle feathers, he had shown cowardice. While the others fought and died in the mud, he had run away into the forest.

Swift Elk had seen him and with his dying breath had repeated the no-retreat chant. '*Tuwa nape cinahan opa kte sni ye.*' Whoever runs away shall not be admitted.

How could a warrior who had fled remain wise in

the ways of the spirits? It was impossible, and yet Matotope was too cowardly to admit his fault. Instead, he'd performed the ceremonies and sought for advice. Advice which had never come since that day in the battle. And so, Matotope had made up the messages and offered to Red Hawk his own poor human wisdom as the Voice of the Great One.

And so the White Water people had died.

'I call upon the Horse!' he cried out. His heart beat with a hollow sound. He willed himself to see and hear the vision sent by Wakanda.

At midday a wind began to blow from the south west. It swept across the open plain to the ledge where Four Winds stood.

The wind was warm and carried with it clouds of red dust which whirled around the boy's face. It tugged at his unbraided hair and whipped strands into his eyes. But still he stood facing the dust storm, arms stretched in prayer.

His stomach was empty now, and his mouth dry. His legs were weak. He stared into the sky, waiting for the messenger to be revealed.

Would it be Elk bringing him the gift of courage? Or the Fox with its cunning? Its brother, the Wolf, for

41

hardiness, or the Night Owl with its wisdom? Whoever appeared would become Four Wind's guide for the rest of his life. He would wear with pride the creature's emblem – feather or claw, tooth or horn.

The wind blew and the sky darkened under the hot, southerly dust storm. The boy stood his ground, though his head spun and the noise of thunder filled his ears. He swayed forward towards the edge of the ledge, unable to see the ground beneath, his heart racing.

'*Wanma yanka yo!*' he yelled above the wind. 'Behold me!'

In a rush of dust and warm air a pale figure appeared above his head.

Through his eyelashes and half-closed lids, Four Winds saw the blurred outline of a four-legged creature. Surely this was his wise spirit, appearing in a cloud from the south. Something large, but not as immense as the buffalo, strong, with a long, graceful neck like the antelope. And long, white hair that fell to one side of the neck, and also formed a flowing tail.

Head swimming, outlines blurred, Four Winds leaned back against Talking Gods Rock.

The creature came and stood beside him. Its large, dark eyes stared calmly into the boy's own.

'I am swift as the Deer, strong like the Buffalo, brave like the Elk. I will not fail you.'

'Who are you?' Four Winds whispered.

The creature tossed his head. 'I am Silver Cloud.'

FOUR

Through the cloud of red dust and the rattle of thunder, the pale horse spoke.

'I am Silver Cloud, sent by Ghost Horse.'

Four Winds pressed himself against the tall rock. He knew this creature. It was the one who had stood on the mountain while he collected water in the wooden bowl. Tall and graceful, separate from the rest.

This dream horse had the same silver grey coat, like morning mist. He carried his head high and

arched his strong neck. His ears listened to all the sounds of the world, his dark eyes saw what was invisible.

Still, the boy didn't step forward. He recalled White Deer's warning that a flower may be beautiful, yet kill with its poison. Was this a good spirit, or one sent by Anteep the wicked chief of the underworld?

He reflected, remembering that he had performed the *inipi* and opened his pure heart to the Great Spirit. He had fasted at the sacred rock. All was as it should be.

Besides, he had been sure on the mountain, across a gap of a hundred paces, that the Great Spirit was present in the pale horse.

'I am Silver Cloud,' the horse said again. The dust storm was dying, the thunder rolling into the distance. 'I will be your guide.'

'My name is Four Winds, of the White Water band, member of the great Sioux nation,' the boy said, his voice shaking. For many winters, since he'd sat among the women in the tipi with warmth from the fire playing on his cheeks, he'd longed for this moment.

'My little Kola, one day you will go out to the sacred rock and seek your dream,' his mother had promised.

'Your vision will guide you and guard you in all that you do.'

Four Winds' fingers lightly touched the lizard skin pouch hanging from his belt. He smiled in gladness at the arrival of Silver Cloud. 'You bring me the wisdom that I need to be a warrior.'

The horse lowered his head. 'Wisdom and courage, strength and speed. I bring all these.'

'*Nagi Ksa pa wan.*' Wise spirit. The boy spoke the words and the beating of wings inside his chest ceased.

'Above all, I bring you loyalty,' Silver Cloud continued. 'I will never fail you. Love sits in my heart.'

Swift as the elk, strong as the buffalo, brave as the mountain lion, loving and loyal like the horse. Four Winds' smile broadened. 'Now I can fight our enemy, the Comanche Wild Dogs!'

Silver Cloud was silent.

'That is the reason for my vision quest,' the boy explained. 'The people of my village are dying in battle. Those who remain are too few. Also, my grandfather, Red Hawk, is old and weak. I must fight in his place.'

Still the dream creature said nothing.

'The medicine of Matotope cannot overcome the troubles of our People,' Four Winds ran on. 'Even his great wisdom fails.'

'All may still be well,' Silver Cloud murmured. 'I bring a message from Ghost Horse. But do not be too eager to enter into battle. Sometimes it is wise to take another way.'

Four Winds went close to the creature. 'I want to be a warrior,' he insisted. 'I wish to walk with my quiver and bow beside One Horn and Running Fox.'

Silver Cloud drew a deep breath through his wide nostrils. He saw the eagerness in Four Winds' eyes. 'Wait. Listen. When I have spoken with Red Hawk who lies sick in his tipi, then you will understand.'

But this answer wasn't enough. 'I must fight Snake Eye on the battlefield. I must fashion my bow strongly and make my arrows fly straight into the hearts of my enemies. In the name of my father, Swift Elk, and that of his cousin, Black Kettle.'

For a moment, doubt crept like a fox into the boy's heart once more. What need did he have of a guardian whose advice would bring shame? For he knew the *Cante Tinz* saying, 'Whoever runs away shall not be admitted.'

'Come.' In turn the boy's eagerness to kill saddened the horse. He began to make his way along the ledge under the shadow of Talking Gods Rock.

Four Winds sighed angrily, then followed on

unsteady legs. Silver Cloud's hooves clattered against the rock until he reached level ground. The harsh, grating sound brought Matotope down from Spider Rock.

The boy saw the medicine man emerge from the settling dust cloud. Matotope's face was weary and smeared with dirt, his body scratched with thorns.

But when he saw the horse, his hand sprang to his wide belt and he drew out his scalping knife. He raised it over his head, ready to ward off the animal's approach.

Four Winds scrambled to the ground and ran between the man and the horse. 'This is Silver Cloud. The Ghost Horse sent him to protect us,' he explained quickly, afraid of the zig-zag blue lines painted along the blade of Matotope's knife. Such a blade, combined with a bear's head carving on its wooden handle, brought instant death.

The medicine man roughly pushed the boy to one side. 'The Horse is the enemy of the Sioux,' he reminded him. 'Once, long ago when ice covered the earth, this creature roamed with the bison and the bear.

'When the ice melted, the bison became our friend, to feed and clothe us. The bear remained and gave us medicines. But the horse vanished into the underworld, along with Anteep, Thadodaho and all the evil spirits and monsters who had roamed the earth. They descended through a yellow pool in the base of a vast canyon, near to the home of Wakinyan, the Thunder Spirit. Now these spirits return only to destroy our People. Be warned, the Horse is a Killer of Men!'

Though Matotope spat out these words and kept the knife raised above his head, Four Winds sprang up. His head reeled from hunger, his lips were cracked by thirst, but he refused to believe what he had just been told. 'Who taught us that the Horse was evil?' he demanded, stepping once more across the medicine man's path.

'It is written in the Great Law.' Matotope jabbed scornfully at Four Winds with his knife.

The boy dodged sideways, then ran to Silver Cloud. 'Speak the words you have spoken to me,' he pleaded.

'I come from the spirit world to guide you,' the horse told the man, looking him in the eye. 'Trust me.'

Slowly Matotope let the knife drop to his side. But a dark scowl remained on his face. 'Give me proof that you were sent by the Great Spirit,' he insisted. He was angry that Four Winds had succeeded on his first vision quest. Jealousy twisted his heart.

'He who asks for proof does not truly open his

mind,' Silver Cloud reminded the shaman. 'The shadow of suspicion clouds his judgement.'

Matotope wondered what to do. Since the creature had first spoken, he knew that Four Winds' search had been successful and that, as usual, his had not. This was what he had feared when White Deer first approached him. If the boy came to the sacred place in purity and simplicity, then surely he would succeed where Matotope himself had failed.

Red Hawk would lose faith. Matotope would look small and foolish in the People's eyes.

But the medicine man carried the sharp tooth of Coyote among the beads and bones of his medicine bundle. He prided himself on his cunning and trickery. So he disguised his jealousy and returned his knife to its beaded sheath. 'You are right,' he told Silver Cloud. 'I see now that I was mistaken. We welcome you as our guide. What message does the Maker of All Things send?'

'Those words are for the ears of Red Hawk only,' the dream horse replied, looking deep into the shaman's soul. 'We must return to your village on the mountain before the sun goes down and rises again.'

Disappointed, Matotope grunted and cast a glance across the desert plain. In the distance, the dust storm gathered on the ridge, rising and smudging the clear blue sky.

'I will take you to speak with Red Hawk,' he agreed. 'If there is still breath in the old man's body, he will hear you.'

FIVE

The journey home took Matotope, Four Winds and Silver Cloud across the plain by day and into the dusk. Through the night they travelled among rocky foothills and by the winding bank of White Water.

As before, the medicine man made his own way in silence, his face guarded, his thoughts more hidden than ever. The silver moon sailed across a cloudless sky; the river ran deep and treacherous.

In the beginning, Four Winds walked strongly. Now he had cast away

childish things and must keep up with the man who walked ahead. Even when Silver Cloud offered to let him ride on his broad back, he shook his head.

'Tell me of the place where the Great Spirit lives,' he said, wanting to hear tales of a world beyond his own.

Silver Cloud began. 'Wakanda lives under the same sun and moon as you,' he explained. 'You can see him in the blue of the sky and the colours of the rainbow.'

Four Winds looked up to the heavens, at the stars and crescent moon.

'And in the night sky,' Silver Cloud said. 'He breathes life into all you see and is not separate from it.'

'He is all around,' Four Winds agreed.

'He binds your spirit to every part of the universe. Your strength, your blood is from the fish and the deer, from the roots and the berries. You were put here beside the White Water by the Great Spirit.'

'He is all around and he is not separate from us,' the boy repeated. He felt cheated of the magical tales his grandmother had told him of a secret entrance to a place where the spirits lived. But he was no longer a child, he reminded himself.

Silver Cloud walked safely by the banks of the rushing river. 'Your grandfather grieves because your

People were born into a place of plenty. While you are in it you fare well, whenever you are out of it, whichever way you travel, you fare worse. The White Water country is in exactly the right place.'

'You know all this?' Four Winds was surprised by the dream horse's understanding.

'It is why I answered your call,' Silver Cloud said simply, waiting a while as the boy struggled between boulders. 'Climb on my back,' he said again. 'The way ahead is hard. There is no one here to see.'

Four Winds looked around and found that Matotope had made his solitary way along a different path. There was a streak of grey dawn in the sky behind them, and a desire built within him to reach the village in the mountains before the sun rose.

So with difficulty the boy climbed on to the creature's back, straddling his weary legs wide and holding tight to a piece of the long white mane. He felt high from the ground and strange.

'You are ready?' Silver Cloud asked.

'I am ready.'

The horse set off at a slow walking pace, aware of the boy's fear. He picked his way with care, sure-footed and steady.

Silver Cloud clutched at the mane as the horse's

55

back rolled. His own body slipped from side to side, his legs hanging uselessly as they moved on.

Because of the night and the lightness of his head, he began to tell himself that this was a dream, riding on a strong creature's back, being carried as if he were a child tied warmly inside a blanket to his mother's back, sleeping while she worked.

The boy and the horse entered the village at dawn. Four Winds was slumped against the horse's neck, floating between sleep and waking.

Dimly aware of the tipis on the hill above, he tried to raise himself. But the trees and rocks spun dizzily and his head lay heavy against the horse.

Around them a cold mist swirled. It swept down from the peaks, across the tipis perched on the mountainside and on into the valley. For a time Silver Cloud and Four Winds vanished from sight, appearing again as ghostly pale grey figures, then melting away in a new surge of cloud.

A hundred paces from the first tipi, Four Winds lifted his head. A sound from behind a rock had startled Silver Cloud and the horse had frozen, ears flat against his head, legs stiff and splayed. Yet, to the boy's dizzy senses there seemed to be nothing there. He urged the horse on.

Still Silver Cloud stood, fixed to the spot between high rocks. He braced his whole body and refused to move.

A loose stone rattled down the hill. The mist came and hid the rocks. When it cleared again, there were five warriors standing high on the rocks, bows strung, arrows aimed at the enemy.

Five arrows aimed at his heart – Running Fox, Little Thunder, Three Bears, Sun Dancer and One Horn! Their bows were strong, their aim true. And they towered over Silver Cloud and Four Winds, their feathered headdresses fluttering in the breeze.

With an effort to steady himself, Four Winds pushed against the horse's neck to raise his body. But weakness overcame him. He fell forward and slipped to one side, feeling his hands lose their grip on the horse's mane. With a slide and a sudden jolt he hit the ground.

And now he was staring up from under Silver Cloud, watching the men he'd known all his life take a new aim at him lying on the earth. He lifted his hand to stop them loosing their arrows.

But the men were afraid. A lookout in the village had come running to their tipis in the grey dawn, telling of the enemy approaching on horseback. The sole Comanche was riding up from the valley surrounded by mist, maybe wounded or sick, though the Horse, the *Shonka Wakan*, was strong. One Horn and the others had taken up their bows and waited behind the rocks.

Four Winds rolled from under the horse. Surely they must recognise him. Facing the ground and hauling himself on to his hands and knees, he felt his arms shake and cursed the weakness of his body. A moment later, his arms gave way and he slumped on the ground once more.

One Horn loosened his bowstring. He saw now that the enemy was young, no more than a boy. And the strange silver grey creature stood alert but not angry, seeming to want neither to attack nor flee. He gestured for the others to lower their aim.

Running Fox frowned. Straining for a clear view of the unknown enemy, he questioned One Horn's decision.

'There is no danger from the boy,' the older brave insisted.

'But from the *Shonka Wakan*?' Running Fox grumbled. 'Why don't we kill it?'

'This horse is not to be feared,' One Horn insisted. He leaped down from the rock and approached quietly.

'Draw your knife!' Little Thunder warned, following him. He took his own blade from its sheath and held it high in the air. 'These creatures are one with our enemy, the Wild Dogs. Do not trust it!'

As the mist swept on and the air cleared, One Horn made out the shape of the boy more clearly. He breathed out and let his body relax. 'Put away your knife,' he told Little Thunder. 'This is no enemy.'

Four Winds heard the man's voice as if from a great distance. He felt asleep yet not asleep, conscious of the cold earth against his face, but not able to say who or where he was. Then yes, he remembered danger, and as the man tried to turn him on to his back, he lashed out with his arm

One Horn took the feeble blow with a smile. He lifted the boy in his arms. 'Run to White Deer's tent,' he called to Sun Dancer. 'Tell her to wake Red Hawk from his sleep. This is the boy, Four Winds, back from his vision quest. And say to her that her grandson has brought with him a strange guest!'

White Deer asked them to lay her grandson in the tipi next to Red Hawk's. She covered him in soft skins and built a fire to warm him.

'Where is Matotope?' she asked.

59

'He did not return,' One Horn replied. 'The silver horse followed us into the village. I have tied him to the cedar tree.'

The old woman nodded. 'He brought Kola back among us. We owe him thanks.'

'I will set the girl, Hidden Moon, to stay by the horse,' One Horn promised. 'It is a strange creature, strong but not angry. It is content to stay close by.'

'Leave me now.' White Deer needed to give Kola medicine. Since Matotope was not here to cure him, she must rely on her own herbs and skills. But she said one more thing to One Horn. 'I believe that this creature is part of the boy's vision quest. Let no one harm him!'

The warrior promised and left the tipi.

'Now, my son, we will make you strong again,' White Deer promised. She stroked the boy's brow and dipped a cloth in pure water from the creek. She wiped his dust-covered face.

So young, she thought. Young and smooth-skinned, with dark lashes closed over his clear eyes. Many times she had sat over him while he slept. She prayed that this would not be the last.

Then she turned to heat a small pot of herbs and water over the fire. Soon a sweet steam rose and she took it to Four Winds where he lay. Cooling the liquid, she dipped in a spoon and trickled the contents between his dry lips. Then she waited.

From his faraway place, Kola tasted the medicine on his tongue. It was sharp yet not bitter. There was a faint sweetness to it. He licked his lips and felt gentle hands pour more liquid into his mouth.

White Deer watched him lick then swallow. She smiled as the boy opened his eyes.

He saw blurred patterns of light and shade, the shape of a face bending over him. He remembered a dust storm at Talking Gods Rock, a wind and thunder overhead. He threw aside the skins and sat upright. 'Where is Silver Cloud?' he demanded.

'Who is this of whom you speak?' White Deer asked, quietly putting aside the dish of medicine. She had already guessed the answer, but she wanted the boy to explain.

'The creature sent by Ghost Horse to guide me. I saw him in my vision. I rode on his back by White Water. Where is he?'

'Hidden Moon is taking care of him. He is tethered by the cedar tree.' The old woman calmed his fears. 'So you succeeded in your quest?' she said with a faint smile.

Four Winds grasped her by the hand. 'Beyond my hopes! The dream horse appeared and spoke to me. He carries a message which he must deliver only to the ears of Red Hawk.'

'Stay!' As Four Winds struggled off the bed, White Deer held him back. 'There is no reason to hurry. Your grandfather sleeps.'

'But when will he wake?' Four Winds could see through the flap of the tipi that the sun was already high in the sky. He wondered if the old man had been sleeping through all the days of his journey to the sacred site.

'He wakes in his own time. When you are old as he is, sleep is a blessing not to be broken.'

'But he must hear Silver Cloud's message!'

'Not now. Soon,' White Deer insisted. 'Rest now. Recover your strength.'

Four Winds realised that no argument he could make would change his grandmother's mind. He lay back on the bed, watching the smoke from the fire curl its way up through the hole in the tipi.

After a while of watching and waiting, White Deer relented. 'You have been patient long enough,' she conceded. 'Now I will go and wake your grandfather.'

The boy got up and went to the door of Red Hawk's

tipi with her. There she bade him wait. As she stooped
to enter, he looked around and noticed the children
staring at him from a distance as if afraid to approach.
The women went about their work of grinding grain
to eat, and over by a tall tree which stood at the heart
of the encampment was his cousin, Hidden Moon,
guarding their guest.

Spotting Silver Cloud, Four Winds went across. The
horse appeared peaceful despite his rope tether, and
there was a look about him which seemed glad to see
that the boy had recovered.

The girl too smiled. 'White Deer's medicine was
good,' she greeted him. 'When One Horn carried
you into the village, the children thought you were
dead!'

'Only hungry and thirsty,' he told her. 'Though I
would have died truly if an arrow had pierced my chest.'

'One Horn is sorry. They believed you were the
enemy because of the creature. They expected to see
you return with Matotope, not with the Horse.'

Four Winds shrugged. 'You are not afraid of Silver
Cloud,' he noted.

Reaching out her hand to stroke the horse's neck,
Hidden Moon shook her head. 'He brought you home,'
she said simply.

Just then, a lookout came running from his high rock overlooking the valley. 'Matotope returns!' he cried.

His call was quickly followed by the appearance of the medicine man himself. Matotope strode up the hill full of news. As the men and women rushed to meet him, he swept them aside. 'I must speak with Red Hawk,' he announced. 'Asleep or awake, I will go to his tent.'

'He has had a vision!' the women whispered.

'The vision will save us!'

'The Great Spirit has spoken!'

Knowing this to be untrue, Four Winds ran to catch up with the shaman. As they approached Red Hawk's tipi, the boy stepped in front of the man. 'Your reason for speaking with my grandfather cannot be so great as my own,' he protested. 'We must wait for him to be ready.'

Matotope's eyes narrowed. His expression said that he would waste no time arguing with the boy. Instead, he thrust him aside and entered the tent.

'The Comanche Wild Dogs have broken camp!' he announced in a voice that travelled through the village. 'They are moving through White Water from the east. Snake Eye has vowed to destroy our People!'

There was a silence, then Red Hawk rose from his sickbed and spoke. 'Who has told you this?' he demanded.

'A scout from our brothers, the Oglala Sioux,' Matotope declared. 'I met with him on my journey back from Spider Rock. He is certain that this is true. The Wild Dogs are only ten days away from our village. With horses it will be less.'

'Name the scout,' Red Hawk said, wanting not to believe. 'Give me the reason that you met him on your journey.'

'His name is Nightcloud. I saw him from a high hill and went to cross his path. He carried this news from the Miniconjou, who gave it to him two nights before.'

As Red Hawk listened and considered, Four Winds peered into the tipi. He saw his grandmother supporting the arm of his grandfather, who stood face to face with Matotope.

'We must prepare to fight,' the shaman insisted. 'Though we may all die, we cannot run in the face of the enemy.'

'I hear you,' the old man sighed. He had wished for more days before the final battle. There was perhaps the hope that the Great Spirit would offer His help. 'What news do you bring from the sacred rock?' he asked Matotope.

The medicine man lowered his gaze.

'Did you speak with Ghost Horse?' Red Hawk insisted, leaning heavily on White Deer's arm.

At this, Four Winds entered the tipi. 'I have brought back a messenger from Talking Gods Rock,' he told the old man proudly. 'Ghost Horse chose Silver Cloud and sent him in a vision to me. He waits outside.'

Red Hawk turned his ancient eyes to Matotope. 'This too is true?' he asked in disbelief.

The jealous medicine man raised his head. 'I spoke with Wakanda from Spider Rock,' he lied. 'We agreed that it was good to send a vision to your grandson. That is how it was!'

Staring at his advisor from under hooded lids, weighed down by the passing of years, Red Hawk shook his head. 'How can this be? Why did the Great Spirit choose a boy over the wisest of my band?'

Angrily Matotope drew his painted knife from its sheath and pointed it towards the roof of the tent. 'I have stated the truth!' he declared, then drew the blade between his lips.

Only Four Winds noticed that the shaman prevented the blade from touching his tongue, as was the custom. It was a false oath he had sworn.

The chief turned to his grandson. 'I will come to the

door of my tipi. Bring me this messenger,' he ordered.

So Four Winds ran quickly to the cedar tree and untied Silver Cloud. 'It is time,' he whispered, leading the horse to Red Hawk's tent.

The dappled grey creature trod lightly through the camp. There was a spring in his stride and the carriage of his head was noble. He came to a halt where all the people had gradually gathered, in front of the chief's lodge.

'You have a message from Ghost Horse,' Red Hawk began.

Silver Cloud nodded. 'He knows your grief,' he replied. 'He is sorry that our kind have been put to evil use by your enemy the Comanches. He would have you know that the Horse is a loving animal who means well.'

Red Hawk bowed. 'When we leave this place of the White Water for the final time, the valley will ring with our cries,' he lamented. 'It will be a terrible howling when we leave the home that has been ours through all time.'

'It may not be so,' Silver Cloud replied.

Matotope stepped forward to interrupt with his dark scorn. 'So Snake Eye and his Wild Dogs will simply turn their horses away? They will give us our valleys back without a fight?'

'I know nothing of Snake Eye,' Silver Cloud said. 'I come only to deliver the message of Ghost Horse and to put to the chief of the White Water band a new path for the future, without hard times and the trail of tears.'

Once more Matotope laughed without gladness from the hollowness of his spirit.

But Red Hawk silenced him. 'For the welfare of my People and the coming generations, I am happy you have come,' he told Silver Cloud. 'Tell me of this new path without tears and how it can be achieved. But remember, our enemies have rolled their tipis on to their travois and their horses move towards us. There is little time.'

It was Silver Cloud's turn to bow. 'Ghost Horse knows this. Still, he promises a way of saving your people without spilling more blood. He will give you the freedom to live in White Water, the land of your forefathers.'

'Show me this way,' the old man invited, a glimmer of hope lighting his features. He held on to White Deer to steady his shaking limbs.

'Ghost Horse has given me a task which I must complete with the help of your People. You must give me the one you love the most to accompany me on a hard and dangerous journey. If you believe in me with all your heart I will not let you down.'

Red Hawk nodded eagerly. He saw nobility in the dream creature and truth in his large, clear eye. 'Say what is the nature of this journey.'

'It will take me through fire and ice, through thunder and the raging waters to the farthest corners of the earth.' Silver Cloud did not diminish the difficulty of his challenge.

'And what is the task?'

'Following the command of Ghost Horse, through whom the Great Spirit Wakanda speaks, my quest is divided into three. Each part must be completed to save your People. First I must bring back to you a diamond from the deepest mine. Then I will search for an eagle feather from the highest mountain and return it here to you. Last, my journey will be to find a breath of wind from the furthest ocean.'

'And if you do this, my People will be free?' Red Hawk's hand shook and his breath came short.

'Ghost Horse says it is so,' Silver Cloud replied. He gazed at the circle of faces - young and old, all wary, each caught between doubt and the desire for his words to be true. 'Trust me,' he told them. 'I came in a vision to the boy called Kola. My heart is true.'

The sun shone from high in the sky on the painted walls of Chief Red Hawk's tipi. Overhead an eagle soared.

'A diamond from the deepest mine?' Red Hawk whispered.

Silver Cloud bowed his head.

'An eagle's feather from the highest mountain?'

'That is the second task of three,' the messenger confirmed.

'And a breath of wind from the furthest ocean?' The old man sighed. He considered the blue of the sky and the green of the valley below.

'Yes. And you must give me the one amongst you whom you love the most,' Silver Cloud reminded him, preparing to withdraw from the circle of onlookers. 'Think now, and before the sun goes down give me your answer.'

SIX

As was the custom, Red Hawk called a gathering of all his warriors. One Horn, Three Bears, Little Thunder, Sun Dancer and Running Fox came to his tipi, along with Matotope and Four Winds.

The women and children watched them with uneasy hearts. Such a council was usually a preparation for battle. From the cedar tree where she watched over Silver Cloud, Hidden Moon saw with pride her cousin, Four Winds, stoop to enter the painted tipi.

Inside the tent, scented

smoke filled the air as a pipe was passed between the men.

Four Winds took in the faces of the braves. There was One Horn wearing the scars of battle with quiet dignity, Running Fox sitting by Matotope, both with thirty summers. They looked tensely at the floor and passed the pipe swiftly between them. Then there was Three Bears with his broad shoulders, the skin of his cheeks and brow tattooed. He was a man who had never known fear. Little Thunder and Sun Dancer were younger, with scarcely twenty summers each, yet their glittering eyes told of things that Four Winds had not yet witnessed.

Sitting in a circle with them, the boy felt humbled.

Red Hawk began to speak. 'You understand well that a spirit horse waits by the cedar tree. You saw the creature come from the valley, from the sacred site called Talking Gods Rock.'

The men bowed their heads and waited. They respected their chief's age and wisdom.

'Silver Cloud travelled with Four Winds to our village. He brings guidance from Ghost Horse, who is close to Wakanda, the Great Spirit.'

Hearing his own name, Four Winds held up his head. He, after all, had been chosen on his first dream quest. He could sit alongside Little Thunder and Sun Dancer without shame.

Across the circle, Matotope looked stern and impatient.

'My brothers, Silver Cloud has described a difficult task. He must face great danger for us and bring back certain sacred objects to bless our band and save us from our enemies. More: I must send the one I love the most to accompany him on his quest.' Red Hawk's gaze travelled around the circle, resting on no one. He knew that each and every one of his warriors would offer themselves for the task, for it would save the People and bring great glory.

In the silence, Matotope took the pipe from the centre of the ring, a signal to speak. 'What if the creature should fail in his quest?' he asked. 'What then?'

Red Hawk listened and showed with a gesture that his medicine man should continue.

'I was present when the silver horse told of his task,' Matotope explained to the rest. 'He must find a diamond from the deepest mine, a feather from the highest mountain and a breath of wind from the farthest shore.'

A murmur went around the circle. Running Fox and

Little Thunder shook their heads.

'We hear from Nightcloud of the Oglala nation that Snake Eye has broken camp and swears destruction on our People,' Matotope continued.

The mood inside the tipi grew darker. This was bad news. Each warrior prepared his mind for the last great battle.

'If we take the advice of the silver horse and wait for his return, Snake Eye draws ever closer. We are few. They are many. Do we sit in our tipis and lay aside our weapons? Do we die in shame?'

'No!' Running Fox declared his opinion without taking the pipe. The word exploded from his lips and he shaped his hand into a fist. 'I will die with my war club raised, not in my tent like a woman!'

'Matotope advises well,' Red Hawk sighed. 'There is this great risk in trusting Silver Cloud.'

Four Winds felt a tightening in his throat. He wished to speak, but he did not hold the pipe, and besides, his thoughts were confused.

He remembered his desire to fight – the pride of battle carried out in the steps of his father, even the thrill he'd felt at the thought of danger. Tomahawk against tomahawk, blade against blade. There was bloodlust in him which could not be hidden.

74

But now it was not so simple. Silver Cloud had said there was another way – a great journey, a seemingly impossible mission. And Four Winds felt honoured by the visitation. His vision quest had succeeded and he'd learned to believe his dream horse. So bloodlust gave way to trust and he was left speechless in the circle.

'There is more to say,' Matotope continued, addressing Red Hawk directly. 'Remember how we spoke together three suns since? We know that the horse bears the enemy of our People on his back, that he has sought our destruction along with the Comanche. You believed that this creature had an evil spirit. How is your mind changed so much since then?'

There was a deep frown on Red Hawk's brow. 'I sent you in peace to Spider Rock,' he reminded the shaman. 'The boy went with you. He was cleansed and his heart was pure. So we must believe that the vision is true and the horse, Silver Cloud, is good. Or what is the worth of our beliefs and the beliefs of our fathers before us?'

One Horn took the pipe and spoke. 'This is right,' he declared in a low, steady voice, his eye upon Four Winds.

'But my heart tells me to follow the wisdom of Matotope,' said Running Fox, seizing his turn. 'I would

75

fight like with like, take out a raiding party while Snake Eye sleeps and seize his horses. With these creatures on our side, we will then have a hope of victory!'

Four Winds glanced at Little Thunder, Sun Dancer and Three Bears. Their faces were set in gloomy lines as the arguments flew to and fro. Inside his own head he held the picture of the silver grey horse. So he took the pipe from Running Fox. '*Nagi Ksa pa wan*. The horse is a wise spirit. I know this. He brings us wisdom and courage, strength and speed, but above all he brings loyalty. Love sits in his heart.'

The boy lay down the pipe in the centre of the circle and no one took it up. His words went deep and moved the warriors.

'Do we wait or fight?' Red Hawk asked at last.

'Fight,' said Running Fox.

'Wait,' said One Horn and Sun Dancer.

'Wait,' said Four Winds, feeling the birds beat their frantic wings inside him.

'Fight!' Matotope cast his vote.

'Fight,' Little Thunder echoed.

All heads turned to Three Bears, who sat in deep thought. He had never been defeated in single combat; he wore the ermine pelts and eagle feathers of a great warrior. He was proud and strong.

'Do we take up our bows against Snake Eye, or do we send Silver Cloud on his quest?' Red Hawk repeated. 'Fight or wait?'

Three Bears kept his eyes closed and head bowed. 'Wait,' he breathed. 'And may the Great Spirit go with him!'

'It is good,' Red Hawk sighed. He had dismissed his warriors from his tent and spoke only to White Deer.

She helped him lie on his bed in the darkened tipi, stroked his brow and soothed him. She saw that the life force had ebbed further. He was an old man clinging to this world hour by hour, minute by minute. But she would not weep.

'Four Winds has done well,' she murmured.

Red Hawk nodded. 'His words must have spoken deeply to Three Bears. For who would have believed that our boldest warrior would hold back from battle?'

'The boy is pure, the horse is true,' White Deer said. 'All will be well.'

So the old man closed his eyes with a peaceful mind. It was good to hold back from sending his braves into what must surely be the valley of death. Instead, Silver Cloud and his companion would guide and save them.

When he woke again, Red Hawk would choose the one he loved the most.

'Who will go with the ghost horse?' the children asked. 'Will it be the strongest among us, or the wisest?'

'Perhaps Three Bears, because he wears most pelts on his war shirt,' one suggested.

'Or my brother, Running Fox, for his swiftness and cunning,' another said.

'But Little Thunder and Sun Dancer are younger,' one of the girls pointed out. 'They will not tire as an older man would.'

Hidden Moon sat some distance away, guarding Silver Cloud. She noticed that the children were no longer afraid of their visitor and that the horse regarded their play with interest. He turned his head to watch them run, swished his long, silken tail and snorted softly.

'One thing is certain,' she murmured with regret. 'Red Hawk will not choose me.'

'Because he does not love you?' Silver Cloud asked.

'No. Because I am a girl.'

Her answer surprised him. 'Amongst my people, this would not be so. Many times the mare is leader of the herd.'

Hidden Moon sighed. 'You will find it strange here.' She looked out to the west at the sinking sun. 'Red Hawk sleeps while the warriors fight to go with you. Look.'

Silver Cloud turned to watch Little Thunder arguing with his cousin, Sun Dancer. The two men had emptied their medicine bundles on to the ground and each was claiming greater power.

'I carry a feather necklace!' Sun Dancer cried. 'With this around my neck, I run light as a feather.'

'And I have this pouch of herbs. When my legs grow weary, I place the herbs in my nostrils and I gain new strength!' Little Thunder boasted.

Sun Dancer seized a bear's claw. 'With this, I can never be weakened!'

'Here is my swallow's head. I fly speedily through my enemies without being touched!' Little Thunder refused to be beaten, and the squabble continued until Matotope himself strode between them.

'Wakanda, I will give you my blood to save my People!' he proclaimed. He made his vow with his right hand raised towards the sun.

His loud voice sent the children running and brought the other warriors from their tipis. Three Bears and One Horn frowned as they approached, while Running

Fox looked puzzled by his former ally's swift change of mind.

'So now Matotope wants to accompany the horse,' One Horn said.

'Only to prove that he is above us all,' Three Bears muttered. 'They say that he consulted the skull from the White Sister Medicine bundle. That skull has great power to tell the future.'

'And no doubt the White Sister Skull foretold that Matotope would accompany the spirit horse on his quest,' One Horn grunted, prepared to show openly his growing dislike of the shaman.

'No doubt,' Three Bears agreed.

'I am most powerful among the White Water People!' Matotope swaggered around the cedar tree, knowing that all eyes were on him. 'I talk with the birds of the air and the four-legged creatures. They tell me their secrets so that no man shall defeat me!'

Until now, Four Winds had been talking quietly with his grandmother, waiting for Red Hawk to wake and give his decision. But the sound of the shaman's bragging brought him running. He saw the tall figure strutting around Silver Cloud, who was tethered to the tree, and immediately he grew angry.

Wasn't this the man who had argued against the

journey? His doubts had almost swayed the vote and sent the warriors into a hopeless stand against the enemy. Now here he was proclaiming himself fittest to be the horse's friend.

Four Winds slipped through the gathered crowd and went to stand beside Hidden Moon and Silver Cloud.

'I will fight the fiercest enemy and slay the monsters of the underworld!' Matotope shouted, his back to Silver Cloud. 'I will guide this spirit creature to the diamond in the deepest mine and I will return it here to you, my People!'

'Good words,' Three Bears grumbled. 'But deeds must follow!'

Matotope challenged him. 'Who has the most wisdom amongst us?' Delving deep into a goatskin bag slung across his shoulder, the shaman drew out a skull covered in green feathers and smeared with sacred red paint. Dark beads glistened in the hollow eye sockets.

Some in the crowd gasped and cowered away.

'Behold the White Sister Skull!' Matotope shouted. 'Through it I hear White Sister prophesying the future. She has told me that it must be I, Matotope, who guides the dream horse on his quest!'

The boastful words took away Four Winds' breath.

Yet who could stand up against the shaman's superior wisdom? Who except for Chief Red Hawk, who was at this moment coming out from his tipi towards the cedar tree.

The boy thought that he had never seen his grandfather look so angry. There was a fire in his pale cheek as he strode ahead of White Deer, who came running after.

'Let the medicine man be silent!' Red Hawk commanded. 'Let this foolishness cease!'

The sight of the tall old man wrapped in a blanket, his white hair braided, his eyes sparking with fury, stopped even Matotope. He had thought him close to death, unable to stand and argue over who should go with the horse. This was why he had come out to swagger and boast.

'I should strike you down with my own war club!' Red Hawk threatened. 'But this old arm is shrunk and I have no strength.'

Matotope drew breath as if to speak.

'Silence! You believe that in my head I am as weak as in my arm? I am Chief Red Hawk still, and though darkness steals over me, I will not give way to empty words and hollow vows!'

'Sit, my husband!' Seeing that Red Hawk staggered,

White Deer drew him towards a rock where he could rest.

He stumbled against Silver Cloud, who stood steadily to support him. 'I will stand!' he insisted, his arm around the horse's neck. 'Matotope, I have long prayed to the Great Spirit for guidance. I have fasted, I have held faith in you, wise man of my band of brothers, even though my People fell on Thunder Ridge and at Burning Rock.'

The chief's great anger held the people in a solemn hush. They looked from Matotope to Red Hawk, seeing the shaman shrink back.

'You have brought false word from the sacred site,' the old man went on bitterly.

'No!' Denial set into the shaman's features to hide his shame. 'I have told only what the spirits said.'

'And would Wakanda lead us into battles we could not win? Would he permit us to be driven from White Water into the wilderness? No, you have betrayed me, Matotope. I see with clear eyes that I have been foolish to follow your word!'

'I will not stand and hear these insults!' the medicine man vowed. He thrust the sacred skull back into its bag and whirled around as if to stride to his tent. He caught a glimpse of satisfaction on One Horn and Three

Bears' faces and snarled at them. 'Who has talked against me?' he demanded. A thought struck him and he turned on Four Winds. 'You have spoken evil of me. It was you!'

Four Winds shook his head. 'I have said nothing.'

'It is so,' Red Hawk insisted. 'Matotope, it is your actions only that have brought this shame. Your wisdom has failed this people since the day in battle at Burning Rock when my son, Swift Elk, fell at your side. I do not know the reason and I do not wish to know. The Great Spirit sees all.'

'I am shaman to this People. They trust me,' Matotope insisted, appealing for friends to step forward. 'Running Fox, speak!'

But the warrior drew back and remained silent.

'Matotope, you will leave this place,' Red Hawk said in a slow, sorrowful voice. 'You will not return.'

The shaman recoiled as if from a sharp knife.

'You will go before the sun sets and speak to no one in this village. From this day we cut all blood ties. You have shown the cunning of the coyote and the venom of the snake, and you are no longer brother to the White Water Sioux!'

SEVEN

The sun set slowly over the jagged mountain tops, turning their snowy peaks pink. At the darkening of the day Matotope rolled up his tipi, loaded it on to a travois and harnessed his dogs to drag it out of the village. Then he slung his medicine bundles across his shoulder and set out.

His brothers shunned him, turning their backs in a show of scorn. The man who had sat at the chief's side had proved false and driven their People to their deaths. There was no forgiveness in their hearts.

The shaman drove his

dogs between the tipis, his head raised in defiance. He was a tall, thin figure, still splendid in his buckskin war shirt which hung with pelts and was trimmed with beads and porcupine quills. But his face was dark and his mouth bitter.

'Where will he go?' Hidden Moon asked Four Winds.

Matotope stalked past the cedar tree where they stood with Silver Cloud. He stared straight ahead, determined to hide his feelings. A man travelling alone at the approach of winter had much to fear from the mountain lion and black bear. And besides, Snake Eye and his Wild Dogs were sweeping across the plains on horseback.

'He will go into the mountains,' Four Winds guessed, watching the two black dogs strain between the shafts of the sled. However, his whole mind was centred on the choice that his grandfather had to make.

'But he will die,' the startled girl said. 'The cold will kill him.'

Four Winds shrugged. It was as it was.

So Matotope was cast out from the White Water people, to perish in the snowy wastes.

The boy stood closer to Silver Cloud while Hidden Moon went in search of warmth from her tipi fire.

She was suddenly cold to the bone in the gathering darkness.

'My grandfather must decide now who will go with you,' Four Winds murmured to the horse. 'There is no putting it off since the sun has sunk behind the mountains.'

'Ghost Horse bid me wait until the North Star appears,' Silver Cloud told him. 'After that I must leave your People and return to the spirit world. You will be left without guidance to face Snake Eye.'

'It is a hard decision.'

'Not to make it is harder still.' The creature spoke kindly, without impatience.

And then White Deer emerged from Red Hawk's tipi. The whole village had been waiting for the flap to be raised and an announcement to be made, so they followed the old woman's movements as she wended her way through the tipis. She came past the painted war tents of Sun Dancer, Little Thunder and Running Fox without looking. Then she seemed to hesitate close to Three Bears' home.

So Red Hawk had chosen the strongest of all the warriors. Four Winds sighed and bowed his head. He felt heavy with disappointment. His grandfather had chosen strength over youth to aid the dream horse in his quest. Had he, Four Winds, ever stood a chance, he wondered.

White Deer looked at Three Bears sitting outside his tipi, his eyes raised towards her. She shook her head and turned away, walking on to meet One Horn, the wisest and boldest of the White Water warriors.

Four Winds watched his grandmother speak with One Horn. He saw by the sag of the man's shoulders that he was not the chosen one. White Deer reached out her hand and touched his arm, then walked on towards the cedar tree.

Flames from the tipi fires played across her face as she approached Four Winds. A wind tugged at her long woven shawl which she clutched close to her chest. And he could see tears in her eyes when she reached him and stopped.

'Kola, you are the chosen one,' she whispered.

The boy stood in his grandfather's tipi and felt his lack of years. He remembered the summers playing on the banks of White Water River, the winters spent in this tipi listening to White Deer's stories of Micabo's Island, when Hare took a grain of sand out to sea and made a small island to keep his children safe from Wolf. When Wolf swam after them, Hare made the island bigger. It grew so vast that even Wolf couldn't find Hare and his family, who lived happily and forever on their beautiful island.

Now he couldn't believe such things. He was a warrior and had been chosen.

'You are young,' Red Hawk began in a solemn voice. 'Your war shirt carries no pelts, your bow arm is untried.'

Four Winds lowered his head.

'Yet I will send you out on this journey to find a diamond from the deepest mine.'

The boy felt his heart jump and jolt. He glanced up and met his grandfather's gaze.

'Many voices counselled me inside my head,' the old man confessed. 'There are those here who are stronger than you, my son, and those who are wiser. I have five warriors who might succeed in this task, in whom I would place absolute trust. Wisdom tells me to choose one among them.'

Standing silently in the background, White Deer wrung her hands.

'Then I listened closely to my heart,' Red Hawk continued. 'Silver Cloud comes from Ghost Horse with a message that tells me to choose the one I love the most. I sought in my heart and cast away anger, bitterness and fear. I let only love remain. Then I slept. And when I awoke, there was only one name on my lips, and that name was Four Winds, the son of my son.'

The boy's own eyes were bright with tears. 'May my arm be strong in the service of my People!' he declared.

'Kola, my boy!' White Deer moaned.

'May your spirit be strong also,' Red Hawk counselled. 'You are my blood, my future. You carry with you the lives of all your brothers and sisters, to make amends for my own foolishness.'

'No!' His wife came forward, determined to speak. 'It was not your foolishness but the treachery of Matotope that led our sons to their deaths.'

'I was weak,' Red Hawk insisted. 'For two summers I have secretly questioned the wisdom of Matotope's war medicine, yet I did not speak out. I have paid for that with the blood of my brothers.'

'And must we also sacrifice our son's son, who is little more than a boy? Must we now send him to his death?' Beside herself, moaning and sighing, the old woman pleaded for Red Hawk to change his mind.

'I will not go to my death,' Four Winds argued. 'I will go with Silver Cloud to fetch the diamond. After that, I will bring back an eagle's feather and a breath of wind. Our people will be saved.'

His words only made White Deer weep the harder.

'Listen, grandmother.' Four Winds spoke again. 'Silver Cloud came to me at Talking Gods Rock. He chose to appear to me there, and now it is right that grandfather sends me on the journey.'

'You say this because your boy's heart is proud. It is a great honour to be chosen. This alone does not make you more likely than another to succeed.'

Four Winds weighed her words. 'I say it is right to be chosen not for that alone,' he insisted. 'But because Ghost Horse demands it. I am the one Grandfather loves the most. Besides, I trust Silver Cloud and he trusts me.'

White Deer looked at him with anguished eyes. 'Kola, there are dangers that you do not know. Evil men and evil spirits will work against you, and your horse protector may not be strong enough to save you.'

But he shook his head and turned to Red Hawk. 'The sun is set,' he reminded him. 'We must leave before the North Star appears.'

The old man nodded and drew the boy towards the fire. 'Come, we must offer a pipe to Wakan tanka.'

Taking up a long-stemmed pipe with his trembling hand, Red Hawk made a rapid chant. 'Wakan tanka, behold this pipe. I ask you to help me.' Then he handed the pipe to Four Winds.

The boy took up the chant. 'Wakan tanka, behold me. I do not want to kill anybody. I only want to save my People. I ask you to help me.' He then returned the pipe to his grandfather.

Red Hawk completed the chant. 'Wakan tanka, I have let my breast be pierced in battle. I have shed much blood. Now I ask you to protect my son's son from shedding more blood. *Wakan yan mica kelo canon pa wan tokeca.* In a sacred manner he made for me a pipe that is different!'

'Now may I go?' Four Winds asked.

'Wait, there is a gift I must give.' Shaking with weariness, Red Hawk crossed towards a wicker box and lifted out his own buckskin war shirt. Adorned with blue and red beads, with a fringe of hair, it was blue on the upper half and yellow below. 'There is honour and authority in this shirt,' he explained to Four Winds. 'I pass it on to you now, my grandson, before my last sun sets. Wear it on your journey and remember me.'

Four Winds took the warm garment and slid it over his head.

Red Hawk delved into the chest and brought out a

second object. 'This is my medicine bundle, which I also give to you, my dead son's son. May it protect you as it has protected me.'

The boy slung the bag around his shoulder and made ready.

'Last of all, take this knife from my medicine bundle. Its blade is sharp, its power great.'

With the knife in its beaded sheath strapped to his waist, Four Winds was at last equipped for his journey. His heart hammered against his ribs, his throat was dry.

'*Maka akanl wicasa iyuha el,*' Red Hawk said from deep in his throat. Go in peace. He grasped the boy's arm and looked steadily into his eyes. Then he released his hold.

Four Winds turned to White Deer. 'You are a mother to me. Give me your blessing,' he pleaded.

'My heart breaks,' she wept. 'It cracks in two.'

'Then I will go without,' he decided.

But, seeing that his mind could not be altered, White Deer quickly dried her tears and followed him across the tipi. 'Kola, beloved child of our only child, we love and honour you above all else,' she said in a clear voice. 'Go strongly, my son, and bring back the diamond. In the name of your father, Swift Elk, and of your mother,

Shining Star, may Silver Cloud guide you and return you safe to our arms!'

PART 2: THE SEARCH

ONE

'We must go,' Silver Cloud said. The sky was clear, a pale moon was rising.

Four Winds turned from the village and its people and followed the horse down the mountainside.

The eyes of the White Water band were upon him, watching his progress. White Deer stood murmuring at her tipi door, while Red Hawk sat inside. He called upon the Maker of All Things and chanted low and long.

'Return soon,' Hidden Moon whispered, though Four Winds and the horse

97

were already tiny figures moving into the valley below. She pictured herself at Silver Cloud's side, setting out to fetch the diamond. She would be brave as any warrior, she would not tire. Now she stood alone on a rock, her eyes glittering, until the travellers faded into the distance.

Four Winds walked close to the horse, breathing in his warm sweetness. He fell into the rhythm of his companion's movement – a slow, even roll with a steady clip of hooves against the hard ground. Soon his eyes were attuned to the fading light.

'The way is long,' Silver Cloud warned. 'When you tire, I will carry you on my back.'

'Later,' Four Winds insisted. For the moment he was glad to walk under the canopy of stars, listening to the small creatures of the bush startle at their approach. A ground squirrel darted out from under Silver Cloud's heavy feet. The eyes of a ring-tailed raccoon glittered from a tree.

'We must travel south,' the horse explained. 'Bear, guardian of the west, has told me that diamonds lie in the hot lands where the sun is strong. They are deep beneath the earth. We will leave the air and descend into tunnels of rock to find the stones that glitter.'

Four Winds' skin prickled at the idea of being closed

in, with the earth resting on his head. But that was far ahead, he told himself. There were many miles to travel before then.

As they gained the valley and trod alongside the river, Silver Cloud grew used to the boy's actions. Studying the slender, black-haired figure closely, he saw that two legs were not so good as four for carrying a creature's weight, but that two arms helped for pulling aside branches and taking hold of rocks and casting them from the narrow gulleys through which they passed. He found that the boy was agile and could swim across water where the current was less strong, and that he could climb nimbly and reach lookouts that his own size and weight prevented.

It took the horse longer to begin to understand the workings of the boy's mind, however. Why, for instance, did he want to walk when it only tired him? The reason seemed to be linked with a thing called pride, which puzzled Silver Cloud. It also amused him to see Four Winds stumble in rocky places where the ground was uneven. Yes, there was no doubt that two legs held you back on a long journey and to be needlessly proud was a kind of blindness.

'Will we cross the plain and pass by Spider Rock?' Four Winds stopped to catch his breath on the bank of the river. He stopped to scoop water into his palm and drink.

'No. Our journey takes us along Thunder Ridge and by Burning Rock, where your father fell in battle.'

Four Winds frowned. 'Snake Eye came in the night and raided our old village. We had thirty men against a hundred Comanches. The blood of our People stained the earth.' He recalled the time of thundering hooves and raised tomahawks. He had hidden in the bushes and watched the slaughter. The world had wept rain, the wind had howled.

In the morning, One Horn, his face freshly bleeding, had brought Swift Elk's war bonnet to him. The warrior had been pale as the grey dawn, except for the slash of scarlet on his cheek. With two hands he had placed the slain brother's headdress across Four Winds' outstretched arms.

'Why does your grandmother give you a different name?' Silver Cloud asked now. He had read the pain in the boy's silence as he drank by the river.

Four Winds broke out of his thoughts. 'Kola? That is my childhood name. It means "friend", and she teases me with it still.'

'Teases?' the dream horse inquired.

'She makes people smile to remember that I was

once a child at her knee, now that I am grown tall.'

'Kola,' Silver Cloud repeated. He waited a while then spoke again. 'It is a good name.'

Little Kola. Little friend. Four Winds stood up and drew in the fresh night air. Moonlight shone on the horse's dappled coat and shot streaks of silver through his white mane. His calm, kind eye looked straight at him. 'You may call me by that name,' he said shyly. 'For I am your friend, and you are mine.'

Matotope stood by the medicine wheel on Thunder Ridge. He had not walked west into the mountains, as the people of his village had expected, but south east towards Snake Eye and his Wild Dogs band. In one hand he held his long shield of buffalo hide, in the other his blue painted knife.

The clear night sky lit up the circles of white stone which marked out the wheel. One spoke pointed south towards Spider Rock, another east, far across the plain. The shaman walked slowly into the centre of the circles and raised both arms high.

'Thadodaho, behold me!' he chanted. 'Oh, priest of death and revenge, great spirit of Anteep of the underworld, come to me!'

A wind blew the fringed sash which he wore across

his bare, broad chest. There were strips of decorated leather around his strong wrists, and a string of sharp mountain lions' teeth hung from his neck. On his head, falling low over his brow, its pelt trailing down his back like a cloak, Matotope wore the hollowed head of a wolf.

'I call upon Thadodaho. I swear bloody revenge on my enemy, Chief Red Hawk of the White Water band of the Sioux nation. Bring death to the People who have flung me out into the wilderness. May their children and their children's children be wiped from the earth!'

In the sky above a low wind moaned.

'Come!' Matotope cried.

The air whirled around him. Dust rose along the ridge and the noise of thunder rolled through the heavens.

The outcast's heart beat louder. The vision gathered force, the spirit of Thadodaho was about to appear.

Out of the gloom a shape appeared. Three times the size of a man, it towered above Matotope. On its head a thousand black snakes writhed. 'Anteep has sent me to hear what you say,' the monster whispered. 'Speak then.'

Terror beat the breath out of the medicine man's

body. He felt that his heart would break through his chest. Yet hot revenge conquered his fear. 'I wish to follow the spirits of the underworld. I will enslave myself to evil, since Wakanda, the Great Spirit, has turned from me.'

Thadodaho's snakes curled and hissed. Their tongues spat venom. Where it fell, it burned into the rock and made it crumble to dust. The monster reached out its claw like that of a giant bear, forcing the shaman to kneel. 'I look into your heart and I see evil has taken root.'

Matotope's wolf head bowed towards the ground. He felt drops of the monster's venom fall on his shoulders and eat through the skin. He flinched but didn't move. 'I hate the White Water people. Their chief is old, weak and foolish, their warriors waste to nothing. And now they have sent a boy of thirteen summers to seek a treasure which will save them!'

Overlooking the shaman's scorn, Thadodaho gripped his arm and raised him from the ground. 'You speak of treasure!'

'A diamond from the deepest mine. It is as Ghost Horse wishes.' He trembled helplessly, knowing that this monstrous vision could slay him in an instant. 'Ghost Horse has sent his messenger, Silver Cloud, to help the boy named Four Winds. If they succeed in their quest, Wakanda will return Red Hawk to his White Water homeland. Snake Eye and his Wild Dogs will be pushed back whence they came.'

A cruel smile crept over the monster's face. 'Don't be afraid. This boy will not succeed, even with his spirit guide.'

Finding himself flung to the ground, Matotope scrambled to his feet and begged for an explanation. 'What is to stop Silver Cloud and the boy from entering the mine?'

'All the serpents, lizards, ghosts, frogs and owls of the Yellow Water,' Thadodaho roared. His breath swept along Thunder Ridge, blasting autumn leaves before it. 'The deepest mine is far south from here, where the sun scorches the earth. There, in the Black Mountains, the water monster whose name is Unktehi keeps guard. His power belongs to the water. Even the spirits of the air cannot trouble him. He is all-powerful.'

This answer pleased the shaman, yet he knew that powerful monsters might still be beaten by trickery. If Silver Cloud and Four Winds could outsmart Unktehi, then the route through the dark earth to the diamond would lay open. 'Will you go with me to this place?' he pleaded. 'That between us we might kill the boy and destroy the dream horse?'

Thadodaho raised a mighty wind to lift him into the night sky. 'Go alone,' he advised. 'There is a strong evil in your heart, bitter enough to poison a boy who has only thirteen summers. Kill him and leave Silver Cloud to me.'

Matotope nodded eagerly, though the wind made him cower against a rock. 'I will go!' he promised.

'I am there already,' Thadodaho hissed from under his halo of snakes. Thunder shattered the night sky and he was gone.

Daylight stole into the valley where Kola and Silver Cloud walked. A small herd of antelope grazing in a green clearing raised their heads and stared at the two intruders. Their strange appearance frightened a young doe, who bounded away and set the others leaping after her. White rumps flashed between the thin trunks of the cottonwood trees, and they were soon gone.

'When the sun rises in the east and climbs in the sky we will leave this valley,' Silver Cloud told Kola. 'We will come out on to a vast plain, where the grass grows like a great ocean. We must cross it as fast as we can. By nightfall we will reach the Black Mountains.'

The boy recognised that this was the horse's way of

saying that he must ride on his back. And now he was
not too proud to accept, knowing that the horse, like
the antelope, could travel at speed across the flat, open
land.

So when the heat came and the hills were behind
them, Kola rode again. Once more he sat astride Silver
Cloud and felt the horse cover the ground at a walk.
The sway of his broad back was easy, though his head
was alert to every movement and sound on the way
ahead.

'Take hold of my mane,' Silver Cloud told the boy as
he prepared to gain speed.

Kola obeyed, seizing the silken white hair and holding
tight. Suddenly the horse picked up his hooves in a
smooth trot which took Kola by surprise, then made
him smile to himself. He was glad there was no one to
see his clumsiness. He wondered for the first time how
the Comanche people had learned to be so graceful on
horseback when they swept to victory in battle.

The thought made him study the problem more
closely. He found that if he kept his torso upright and
sat down deep in the curve of Silver Cloud's back,
leaving his legs relaxed, then the motion of his own
body didn't fight against that of the horse. In fact, he
was riding smoothly again, finding his balance and

letting Silver Cloud take a longer stride.

'At last!' the dream horse commented. The jolting on his spine had bothered him. 'Now can we go faster still?'

Kola took a deep breath then agreed. He took in the sea of grass ahead and what looked like small clouds gathering on the horizon.

'If you fall, land softly,' Silver Cloud warned. 'Choose a place where there are no rocks and plenty of grass!'

The horse broke into a lope, rocking to and fro in a motion that ate up the ground beneath his feet. His tail streamed out behind, his head was thrust forward, ears pricked to pick up hidden signals ahead.

A thrill went through Kola's body. This was how it felt to be an elk or deer running free across the plain. And now, quite close and growing louder, he heard the beat of buffalo hooves cutting across their path. So it had been dust gathering on the horizon, not rain clouds – a huge herd of bison moving over the land.

The boy knew how these great animals travelled. There would be many of the huge, woollen-headed, horned creatures gathered together, as far as the eye could see. Their passing would not be quick, unless they stampeded, and then there would be danger for all in their path. 'We should choose another way,' Kola advised Silver Cloud, who had also recognised the herd.

'Why? The buffalo is a friend to your people.'

'That's true. Their meat is our food. With their skins we clothe ourselves and build our tipis. They are givers of life.'

'Then we can meet with them without fear,' Silver Cloud decided. Instead of slackening his pace, he broke into a gallop which made Kola feel as if they were flying through the air.

A warm wind caught in the horse's white mane and in the boy's braided hair. Kola leaned low over Silver Cloud's long neck and held tight.

Soon they could pick out small groups of buffalo grazing apart from the main herd. The creatures raised their heavy heads to sniff the air and went back to their sweet, dry grass. Then Kola and Silver Cloud were in amongst them, surrounded by the flat-backed creatures whose hooves raised a cloud of grey dust wherever they went. Kola felt the heat rise from their bodies, could almost reach out and touch their tough black hides, except that Silver Cloud picked his way swiftly between them, leaving Kola no time.

At last they were through the herd and travelling on. A faint outline of hills appeared in the distance and a new river snaked across the plain. 'Are those the Black Mountains?' Kola asked eagerly.

Silver Cloud said that they were. 'The first place we come to is Crow Ridge, and after that is Burning Rock. Beyond the foothills, the Black Mountains begin. And there, in a great canyon, is Yellow Water and the entrance to the deepest mine.'

Kola felt his heart race. He wondered about the dangers that the dream horse had described. Where were the storms, rock falls and fires that came out of the mountains? Might they still have to face these, and waters that roared? For the moment, all was calm and the sun shone over their heads.

At midday, Silver Cloud drank from the river. He rested amongst willows while Kola strode up a grassy hill and stared towards the mountains.

The boy tried to make out details among the jagged, pale purple hills. His keen eyes saw snow on the highest peaks and many dark shadows that meant deep canyons split the rock. But he didn't remember in which of the foothills his father had died.

His attention was caught by a movement far to the east. A spit of rock rose from the plain and formed a low ridge along which a large creature was moving. Kola shaded his eyes from the sun and looked more closely. Could it be a buffalo cut off from the herd? Perhaps an elk which had wandered far from the highland passes?

But the boy saw with a shock that it was a man on horseback, who had stopped his brown-and-white mount to stare across the prairie in his own direction. Kola shrank back as he realised that he might have been spotted by one of Snake Eye's men. He was about to run and warn Silver Cloud when a second figure appeared on the ridge.

This man was on foot. He drew the rider's attention and walked towards him, demanding to be heard. The rider stopped to listen and look in the direction in which the second man pointed. Something in the manner of both figures suggested urgency.

Then after more talk, during which the rider seemed to forget all about Kola, the man on foot vaulted on to the back of the horse. Both were now mounted, turning down the ridge on to the flat grassland, where they set the horse off at a gallop towards the mountains.

The boy stayed just long enough to make sure that they didn't wheel back and pick up his trail. When he saw that their path was straight, he ran down to the river to join Silver Cloud and describe what he'd seen.

But his companion had other things on his mind.

His head was up and he was smelling the air attentively, looking towards the grassy hill and the spit of rock beyond. 'Did you see fire up there?' he asked the boy.

Kola shook his head. 'I saw two men.'

'There is smoke in the wind,' Silver Cloud insisted. He told Kola to climb on his back and together they went up the hill.

This time, when Kola looked towards the spit he did see smoke. A thin trail rose from behind the rock and drifted on the wind until it entered his nostrils.

'The men set a fire,' Silver Cloud concluded. 'It will reach over and around the rock, and eat all in its path.'

Sure enough, the smoke soon thickened and curled around the spit of high land. Flames appeared, licking at the dry grass and roaring as they consumed sagebrush and willow. Wind buffeted the fire, feeding the flames, which now rose three men's height into the air and advanced towards Kola and Silver Cloud.

Kola felt fear twist inside his belly. This meant that the Comanche enemy had spotted them and chosen fire as their weapon to drive the travellers back. Already the smoke had entered his lungs. The wind carried fire faster than any animal could run; the flames ate trees and left nothing but charred black land.

Silver Cloud was also afraid. Fire was the thing which

a horse feared above all. It choked and blinded, roared in the ears, ate flesh. So his instinct told him to flee in the face of flames. 'Hold tightly,' he ordered, whirling around, only to discover that the fire had run quickly along the river bank and cut off their retreat.

Water would have saved them. They could have swum across the river and watched in safety as the land on the opposite bank burned. But the sly Wild Dogs had judged the wind correctly, knowing that their victims would first seek the higher land as a lookout point, before they withdrew to the river. By then, the flames would have surrounded them and there would be no escape.

Silver Cloud carried Kola down the hill, towards the only gap in the flames. A screen of hot, black smoke met them, too thick to see through. The horse put his head down to the ground, feeling Kola fall forwards on to his neck but still cling on, as they made for the ever narrowing gap.

Orange flames licked and roared. They were all around, the ground crackling and sparking, the sap from the trees hissing and spitting. Overhead, a huge plume of smoke gathered.

Silver Cloud galloped on through the scorching heat. There was still a way out, if only they could hold their breath long enough. Behind and to either side, the flames leapt. Tall trees cracked and their burned branches crashed to the ground.

Kola felt sparks shower down on him. He saw Death hold out his hand in welcome.

And then Silver Cloud was through the dark gap, clear of the circle of fire. The flames were behind and they were galloping on, almost blind, sucking in clean air at last. Rocks towered to either side, fencing them in, and a barrier of trees slowed them to a trot.

Kola raised his head from the horse's neck and took in the narrowing cliffs, the slender trees reaching skywards from their gloomy canyon. He felt Silver Cloud slow to a cautious walk through the cottonwoods, saw tumbleweed roll and drift against the bare rock walls. Then the shadows closed in and the horse and the boy came to a sudden halt. A cliff cut across their path.

They turned to see giant flames engulf the rocky entrance to the canyon. Smoke billowed behind them and tongues of flame reached into the gulley. There was no way out.

TWO

Now Kola experienced the true meaning of fear. He was a boy who had known hunger and thirst, the cold of the snow and the glaring heat of the summer sun. He had seen killing and he had hidden in bushes to escape being killed. But still he wasn't prepared to meet death by fire.

He gasped when he saw the flaming entrance to the canyon and slid from Silver Cloud's back. His first thought was to find a way to climb to safety.

The dream horse saw the boy dart in panic to the cliff and search for

footholds. He glanced upwards towards a deep overhang. Climbing was no solution, even for a boy with nimble hands to grasp the rock. For a creature with four legs, the way was impossible.

It was time to call on help from the spirit world, he decided. If the *kachinas* came quickly, then all might be well. So he spoke through the thickening smoke to the spirits of the air. 'I call to the clouds and the rainbows, bring me speedily to he who wears a mask of green jade, bring me to Olmec, the great spirit of the desert!'

Straight away a fresh wind came to hold the flames at bay. It blew strongly down the canyon and fought against the fire. With it came a gathering of white clouds overhead and an arching rainbow of reds, yellow, green and blues.

Silver Cloud stood in the bottom of the canyon, grateful to the friendly air spirits, the *kachinas* upon whom he had called. He watched their clouds grow thicker and thanked the power of Olmec, half jaguar, half man, he of the jade mask who lived in the south. 'Give us rain to kill this fire,' he pleaded, 'for our journey is great and our enemy strong.'

The cool wind blew. Kola looked up from a narrow ledge and saw the rainbow, saw the magic of the sky and a faint jade face in the clouds. He clung to the rock in awe.

'Bring us rain!' Silver Cloud called to the powerful spirits of the air.

The invisible *kachinas* heard and breathed raindrops into the clouds. The drops began to fall on the baked earth inside the canyon. They spattered on the dry rock and in the leaves of the trees. Then they fell faster and a wind drove them down the gulley towards the flames. The hot earth hissed, the host of rising sparks was deadened.

Kola felt the cold rain on his hands and shoulders. He turned his face from the sky to watch the battle between rain and fire at the entrance to the canyon.

'More rain still!' Silver Cloud pleaded. The flames had fought back with a hot roar that had reached them and made them cower against the rock. Kola closed his eyes.

The separate drops became a drenching torrent, blown in sheets by the breath of a thousand *kachinas*. The fire died back, flared up and fought again in the shelter of boulders and overhanging ledges.

But both Kola and Silver Cloud knew that the flames were weaker, that they might dart through the dry grass and catch at tumbleweed, but that the water would defeat them. They heard the angry hiss of the dying flames, saw the grey, powdery ash turn black under the downpour.

They breathed freely, watching the rain ease and the rainbow fade from the sky.

Matotope looked down with disgust as the boy and the horse travelled on through the scarred landscape.

He stood alone on Crow Ridge in the foothills to Black Mountains, awaiting the arrival of Snake Eye.

For now, the shaman's anger concentrated on Anteep's servant, the serpent-headed monster, Thadodaho, who had promised that Silver Cloud and Four Winds' quest for treasure would end in failure.

After his chance meeting on the plain with Snake Eye's scout, Wicasa, Matotope had had high hopes. He had told the Wild Dogs' messenger that a boy from the White Water band was travelling across the plain by horse. Wicasa had gone to his chief and told the story of the boy's journey to the deepest mine. And Snake Eye had swiftly devised a plan to destroy the travellers with fire.

Matotope had taken delight in the grim death which lay in wait for the grandson of Red Hawk.

But then he had watched the rainbow appear in the

sky and immediately he had known that the *kachinas* were at hand. The rain had fallen and Thadodaho, for all his fine words on Thunder Ridge, had done nothing to prevent it.

So now the shaman had demanded to meet the great warlord, Snake Eye, face to face. If the evil spirits would not provide the power that was needed, then Matotope's revenge must be completed by the hand of man.

He grew impatient as he waited, knowing that Silver Cloud and the boy were moving on, growing closer to the mine by the Yellow Water. His memory flitted back to the arrival of the spirit horse at the sacred site, how his heart had twisted with envy of the boy. Then he recalled Silver Cloud's message from Ghost Horse, and how it had happened that Four Winds had been chosen above him once more. There was disgrace in that and shame had pierced him.

The sun sank low in the west as Matotope bitterly remembered. He forgot that he had tricked Red Hawk with false wisdom and dwelt only on the black anger he had felt when his chief had exiled him for ever.

How long would proud Snake Eye keep him waiting here? Was this another insult to add to all those that had been heaped upon him? With narrowed eyes and a deep scowl, he awaited the approach of horses' hooves.

The Black Mountains loomed larger as Silver Cloud and Four Winds left the plain and entered the foothills. They were no longer a hazy purple, as from a distance, but a dark red like the red of war-paint smeared on the faces of Comanche warriors. The shadows lengthened and the air grew cool.

Silver Cloud entered the mountains after a long day spent crossing the plain. He and Kola had survived the fire set by the Wild Dogs, but the effort had tired them both. Fear had drained their energy, and still the acrid smell of smoke lingered. It was in his coat and mane, and on the clothes of the boy – a charred, dead smell that brought back to mind the leaping flames of the canyon.

They needed to sleep, but the mountains offered little shelter. Trees were scarce, scattered up the rocky slopes, their roots twisting out of the dry, crumbling earth. Deepening shadows of rocky pinnacles spread across the narrow valley, and overhead a black raven soared.

'We must rest at the first water,' Silver Cloud told Kola. 'We have journeyed through the night and the day without food. Now it is time to stop.'

Reluctantly Kola agreed, sliding to the ground and easing his legs. They would find a place by a creek and he would pick berries. Grass would be there for the horse to eat. 'Tomorrow will we reach the lake called Yellow Water?' he asked anxiously.

'Perhaps.'

'How deep into the earth must we travel?'

'We will not know until we arrive.' Silver Cloud's ears picked up the sound of running water to the east. As he made his way towards the water, he warned the boy that there were many obstacles still to overcome. 'I must tell you of evil spirits guarding the place, and of Unktehi, the water monster who lives below the lake. He will not let us pass without challenge.'

'Does he guard the diamonds?' Kola asked.

'Yes, he and his spirits bar the way. Many men have tried to enter, but most die at Unktehi's hand. The others return to their People with empty eyes and horror fixed in their hearts.'

Kola felt his courage flicker and fade.

The horse saw this. 'Don't be afraid. I am here to guide you.'

'Then I will be strong,' the boy decided.

But that night, as he lay on the ground beside the creek, staring up at the stars, his heart would not be still.

* * *

'Give me a reason why I should trust you.' Snake Eye drew Matotope towards the fire burning inside a circle of stones. His face was painted white with narrow black streaks running from his forehead to his chin. A slash of red crossed his mouth and stretched from ear to ear.

His men had ridden to Thunder Ridge and seized the shaman. They had bound him with strips of hide and dragged him back to the camp behind their horses. Then they had shown him, bleeding and covered in dirt, to their chief.

'Take off these ropes!' Matotope snarled. Wicasa, the messenger, had betrayed him with false promises of a meeting on the ridge. Instead of Snake Eye himself, a group of four young riders had returned and overcome him. Now all of the Wild Dogs band had gathered round the camp fire to look and listen.

'Give me good cause,' Snake Eye repeated, taking his knife from its sheath. He dug the blade into the earth and studied the outcast closely.

'I come with news of the White Water People, to tell you of their plan to defeat Snake Eye and send him back across the plains.

'Ha!' Grey smoke rose from the fire and hid the

122

chief's face. But there was scorn in his voice. 'Red Hawk has few warriors, his People are weak. Soon Snake Eye will drive them into the snow and they will die there.'

Matotope felt the leather strips bite into his wrists. There were many men here who would raise their knives and strike. He must talk with a smooth, silver tongue to escape death.

'That was so,' he admitted. 'But now there is a dream creature sent by Ghost Horse. Wicasa has seen him, your People have set fire to the grass to drive him back.'

Snake Eye looked around the circle, at men with braided hair and painted bodies. Beyond the thin screen of smoke, their faces scowled with suspicion at the disgraced shaman. The chief picked out his scout who sat cross-legged, leaning on the long staff of his tomahawk.

Wicasa nodded and said this was so. 'The dream horse brought rain from the *kachinas* to quench the flames. He travels south into the mountains with a boy.'

Quickly Matotope laid out more facts. Then he demanded a second time to be untied. He felt that here, in the heart of the enemy camp, he could seal new alliances that would lead to his final revenge.

Snake Eye gestured to the nearest man, who leaned forward and cut roughly through the bonds. The news that the White Water band had earned the help of Ghost Horse troubled him. Now his plan to drive Red Hawk into the mountains would not be so easy. 'Why do you, medicine man to the White Water People, come here to tell me this?' he demanded.

'They are no longer my brothers,' Matotope said hastily. 'They have poured shame upon me and my thoughts are black.'

'You would help us?' The red slash across Snake Eye's mouth stretched into a cruel smile. His hair hung in many beaded braids. He wore crow feathers at his waist and a loincloth of antelope hide.

Matotope raised his head proudly. 'Without my help you will fail,' he warned.

Snake Eye let a silence hang in the smoky air. He knew there was no honour in this man, and yet he could be useful. So he bade one of his men to begin a slow beat on his drum. Another, who wore a cap of wolfskin and rings of silver in his ears, chanted in a low voice.

The rest rose and began to dance, raising their arms to the night sky, calling on Anteep, great spirit of the underworld.

'Come,' Snake Eye said to Matotope, guiding him towards his tipi. 'We will speak more.'

THREE

Two nights had passed and now the sun rose on the second day of Silver Cloud and Four Winds' journey. Instead of open plain they faced narrow canyons between rugged cliffs. For soft grass underfoot there was stone and dust.

Kola woke from a shallow sleep. His dreams had been filled with suspicion and uneasy dread of creatures invented by his own imagination. The monsters were shadowy beings who lurked in the darkness. They had sharp teeth and claws, matted hair and slimy, scaly skin.

They crushed their prey between powerful jaws.

So his head spun and his limbs ached when he stood to find the silver horse already feeding by the water's edge. The sight of him helped calm the boy, who recalled Silver Cloud's promise that he would never let him down.

The horse was graceful in its habits. Every swish of his long tail and twist of his supple neck were beautiful to behold. How could such a noble animal harbour disloyalty?

More ready now to continue the quest for the diamond, Kola went down to the water where he washed his face and drank deeply. He seemed to Silver Cloud vulnerable as he stooped there. A boy, not yet fully grown, with smooth skin and dark, clear eyes. His body still had to put on muscle, his legs were as long and thin as a colt's. And yet Red Hawk had honourably chosen him for this journey, according to the condition that Ghost Horse had laid down. It had been the greatest sacrifice that the old man had had to make, to risk the life of his only son's son. The grandmother had wept bitter tears.

Silver Cloud gave Kola time to finish bathing then search for berries and roots to fill his stomach. At last he told him that it was time to move on. 'We have far to travel,' he reminded him, inviting the boy to climb on his back. 'Yellow Water lies in the heart of these mountains, at the bottom of a canyon so vast that it seems the whole world must split in two. It is a hard journey in the heat of the sun.'

Kola prepared himself. By now he had grown used to the sensation of riding the horse and felt that by minute changes of balance he had become part of the creature's rhythmical motion. There was a harmony between them now.

Silver Cloud's hooves clipped against stones and crunched over sandy gravel. All around, sharp pinnacles of rock rose, their layered bands making strange patterns on the silent landscape. This was no place for antelope or buffalo, Kola thought, but for small lizards basking in the sun and for snakes who hugged the shade.

Yet he felt after a time that he and Silver Cloud were being observed. He would look up at the nearest ridge and there would be no one there, only a suspicion that hidden eyes were looking down on them. This went on for many hours, as the fierce sun went on climbing in the deep blue sky.

At last Kola confided in Silver Cloud. 'There are

eyes in the mountains. I don't see them, but I feel them.'

'You are right,' the horse agreed, without showing any concern. 'A man has followed us since dawn.'

Kola's gaze raked the horizon. The observer, whoever he was, was softer than a shadow, swifter than the wind. There was nothing to see except ravens wheeling overhead.

'He is to the west, in the shade of the overhang. He knows the mountains well,' Silver Cloud observed, as calmly as before.

The boy shot a look in that direction. The overhanging rock was only two hundred paces away. 'What does he want?'

'We cannot tell until he has spoken with us.'

'When will that be?'

'When he chooses.' Silver Cloud stopped, perhaps to invite the hidden observer to show himself.

As the heat beat down upon them in the still air of the canyon, Kola grew afraid in spite of Silver Cloud's untroubled words. Who but the Wild Dog Comanches knew they were here? Why would anyone shadow them without showing himself? Slowly wrapping his fingers around the carved handle of his grandfather's knife, he grew ready to use it.

But almost before he prepared, the man appeared from under the overhang. With hair braided simply, wearing no war paint or war shirt, but only fringed deerskin trousers and soft moccasins, he bounded down from the shady rock into the full light of the sun.

Kola saw at a glance that this could not be one of Snake Eye's men. No enemy would show themselves in this way without wielding a tomahawk or bow and arrow. Nor would he be alone.

'I am Nightcloud of the Oglala Sioux!' the man announced. 'I am your brother.'

Thankfully Kola removed his hand from his knife. He relaxed as Silver Cloud walked up to the man called Nightcloud, who was nimbly scrambling down the rocky slope to meet them. 'You bring us news from the Oglala People?' he asked.

Nightcloud nodded. Hardly breathless, he offered the hand of friendship to Four Winds. 'It was I who sent word to Red Hawk to warn him that Snake Eye had broken camp.'

'I remember.'

'I watched the Comanches and their horses, knowing that they planned to sweep west into the mountains beyond White Water.'

'My grandfather thanks you,' Kola told him. 'But this is nothing new. What else?'

Nightcloud frowned. 'Now I am puzzled,' he confessed. 'The Wild Dogs rolled up their tipis and began to head west as I expected. But then they changed direction. Snake Eye ordered a new camp by Thunder Ridge. He sent men to set flames to the grass and make a great fire.'

'He hoped to trap Silver Cloud and me,' Kola explained. 'But he did not succeed.'

'This I also saw,' Nightcloud said, looking with respect at the dream horse. 'But surely this would not be enough to delay Snake Eye more than one day in his eagerness to defeat your People. Yet still he stays by Thunder Ridge and does not move west.'

The news surprised Kola. He decided to trust his cousin, Nightcloud, by telling him of the reason for his journey with Silver Cloud. 'The lives of my People depend upon our success,' he explained. 'With the diamond, we will be stronger. And then we will bring back the feather and the breath of wind, and Snake Eye will have no power over us.'

'Then the Wild Dogs have learned this,' Nightcloud pointed out. 'Why else would they delay over a mere boy and one horse?'

'But how could they know?' Kola felt a cold shock run through his body. His skin began to sweat.

Nightcloud shook his head. 'I only tell what I see. I watch from afar, I do not listen to their reasons.'

Kola thought hard. 'If you, Nightcloud, can follow our trail, then so can Snake Eye,' he said slowly.

'Yes, but I have not seen Comanches enter the Black Mountains,' the Oglala scout assured them. 'I have waited since dawn for them to follow you, but no man has set foot in these canyons. My warning is only that Snake Eye rests by his tipi and has not travelled west.'

'We thank you,' Kola told him. The bad news meant that he and Silver Cloud must hurry ahead. 'We hope that one day the White Water People will be able to repay our debt to our Oglala brothers.'

Nightcloud bowed his head. He had treated Four Winds as an equal, yet he wondered at his youth. To learn that the future of Red Hawk's band sat upon the shoulders of an untried boy had caught him by surprise. It was news he must take back to Skidi, leader of his band. Raising his head again he spoke the words that meant, 'May the good spirits guide you,' then he stepped back and melted into the shadows.

* * *

133

Four Winds and Silver Cloud journeyed on towards the great canyon in the heart of the Black Mountains. Water grew scarcer as the creeks dried to narrow trickles, and nothing except cacti grew in the sandy earth.

Silver Cloud knew that in the heat of the early afternoon Kola was tiring. He sensed too that the scout's message had raised fresh fears and that the boy was tensely waiting for the Wild Dogs to appear. So he thought to amuse him with a tale.

'There was once a Chief who had a vain and beautiful daughter called Proud Girl,' he began. 'The father chose for her a husband whose name was Bold Eagle.'

'I have heard this story at White Deer's knee,' Kola interrupted impatiently. 'It is for children when they sit around the fire.'

'And for weary travellers and all who care to listen,' Silver Cloud instructed. 'There is laughter in the story to raise a smile, and to carry us on our journey.'

So Kola let the horse continue.

'But Proud Girl did not want Bold Eagle for a husband, though he was serious, strong and brave, and each eagle feather in his headdress signified a bold deed. So she taunted him and called him a man of ice who could not smile.'

134

Talk of ice made Kola long for frozen mountain streams to slake his thirst and cool his skin. He sighed and listened as the story unrolled.

'Still, her father arranged the marriage between Proud Girl and Bold Eagle. But Bold Eagle thought he would have revenge for being called a man of ice. He went out and sang six Power Songs, to the north, south, east and west, and to the sky and the earth beneath. Then he took stones and animal bones, and around them he kneaded snow into the shape of a man. He dressed the man-shape in a beaded shirt and a robe of coloured feathers. He gave him bracelets for his wrists and a splendid headdress, then told him he was the mighty chief, Moowi. "You are rich and handsome," he said to the ice-man. "And no woman can look upon you without longing." '

'I remember!' Kola interrupted eagerly this time. Already a smile played on his lips. Though the story was an old one, he found that it took his mind away from present dangers. 'Though women loved him, Moowi had no heart, no love and no pity. Bold Eagle sent him to Proud Girl's village and watched her fall in love with Moowi!'

'Moowi spoke little, and was cold and haughty,' Silver Cloud went on, glad that his tale had won his rider's attention. 'But still Proud Girl went to her father and demanded to marry him, and her father agreed. There was a wedding feast which Bold Eagle attended. He watched with interest, noting that Proud Girl continued to scorn him. And he smiled when Moowi refused to be drawn close to the camp fire.

'The next morning Moowi and his new wife set out on a journey to the far north, as if to meet his People. He walked swiftly over mountains and through rivers, and Proud Girl wore out her moccasins running to keep up. She grew cold in the wind and snow and begged to rest, but Moowi would not hear of it.

'As long as the snow fell and the wind blew from the north Moowi walked strongly, but then the sun shone through the dark cloud and he began to tire. At last he sat down in the shade of a tree. "My husband, are you sick?" cried Proud Girl.

"Yes, wife, I am very sick," he replied.

'So she ran to a stream to fetch water, but when she returned the sun shone strongly on the tree and there was no sign of her husband.'

'Proud Girl called Moowi's name!' Kola jumped in, his eyes sparkling as he remembered the end to the tale. 'She searched and called out, but found only a little pile of bones and stones and some rags, beads and feathers. So she cried and went home, thin and hungry and no longer beautiful.

'And as she passed by Bold Eagle she saw him smile. "Is it anything to smile at?" Proud Girl asked through her tears. "Yes, it is something to smile at," Bold Eagle replied. And he took his dog and his sledge, and he went back to his own tribe.'

Time passed this way, with more tales and reasons to smile, so that Kola forgot his fears and told Silver Cloud Sioux stories which he had not heard. The sun was high in the sky and Kola had ceased to suspect every rock they came to and every shadow down every dry and dusty gulley.

It was only when the two came to a stream running deep through a narrow gulch that they began to pay attention to their surroundings once more. They each took the chance to drink, then went quickly on, finding to their surprise that the path of the stream was blocked by a giant boulder. The boulder dammed the stream so completely that the water had been forced underground, and beyond this spot, the bed ran dry through the gulch and out into a wide valley.

'What is this place?' Kola asked, looking round the huge, dish-shaped area and picking out deep holes in the sides of the cliffs.

'This is Kooyama,' Silver Cloud explained. 'Home of the cave-dwellers.'

Kola was astonished. He was used to the wind blowing around the skin cover of a tipi on the open plain and had never heard of such a thing. 'The people make their homes in the rock? But they must live surrounded by earth on all six sides. It is all around them, above their heads and beneath their feet!'

Silver Cloud agreed that it was strange. 'We will meet the people as we pass through,' he predicted, moving closer to the holes carved into the rock.

There were a hundred square entrances linked by stone steps and walkways – a village built into the cliff. Each was finely decorated with carvings and inlaid with rich turquoise. But instead of finding that Kooyama's cave-dwellers came out of their strange honeycomb of houses to investigate the strangers, Silver Cloud and Kola discovered that the caves were empty and the whole valley deserted.

'Where are the people?' Kola asked, peering up at the dark entrances. There was no smoke from fires, no dogs barking or children playing.

'Gone away?' Silver Cloud suggested.

Kola thought of a worse possibility. 'Perhaps they are dead.'

'I have not heard.' His guide too was puzzled. Here and there he saw small pieces of broken pottery lying on the ground, and stone circles containing the ashes of long-dead fires.

'Maybe Snake Eye has been here too,' Kola went on. He didn't like the stillness of the air and the thick layers of yellow dust lying undisturbed on the walkways.

'There is no blood,' Silver Cloud pointed out, 'and no sign of battle.' He thought back to the boulder which had dammed up the stream. 'No, I think the water to the village has been taken away. The Kooyama people could not live without water, and so they were forced to move on.'

Sadly Kola accepted the explanation and sympathised with the people. 'They have lost their homeland, the place where they belong.' He wondered long about a tribe like his own White Water band who must wander without roots, and how the boulder had arrived to dry up their water supply. Perhaps it had been angry spirits determined to teach the cave-dwellers a lesson who had dropped the giant rock from the sky.

In any case, there was no time to linger. The sun had run more than half its daily course and the shadows were lengthening. They had to leave Kooyama Valley and press on towards the south.

Kola was glad to be away from the deserted village and travelling on to their goal. As Silver Cloud trotted briskly through the next narrow canyon, he was wrapped up in thoughts of the diamonds which lay deep under the ground beyond Yellow Water. He tried to picture the size of the precious white stones and wondered how they would find their way down the tunnels without light to guide them. And he remembered White Deer, his grandmother, waiting at home, the five warriors around their fires, and Red Hawk lying ill on his bed.

The cry, when it pierced the silence of the valley, froze Kola's blood. It came from the back of the throat, full of bloodlust, filling the heavy air.

He looked to right and left, saw men driving their horses down the hills into the canyon, carrying shields, wielding tomahawks. The boy's heart stopped dead, then restarted with a rapid, uneven beat.

The Wild Dogs were upon them before they had time to flee – six men in full war cry descending at a gallop, trapping Silver Cloud and Kola.

The horse reacted in an instant, rearing up in front of the first warrior to attack. His flailing hooves sent the Wild Dog sprawling from his horse, leaving a gap for Silver Cloud and the boy to charge through.

But the five other riders were in hot pursuit. One launched his tomahawk as they charged. Kola felt it fly close to his head, saw it strike a rock and fall harmlessly. He glanced over his shoulder to see the enemy horses bunch together down a narrow gulley, jostling each other as their riders urged them on. Then he let go of Silver Cloud's mane with one hand and quickly seized his knife.

Ahead, the gulley widened and the Wild Dogs spread out. They raced alongside Silver Cloud, leaning to swipe at Kola with their tomahawks. Swiftly Silver Cloud swerved to avoid them.

With an extra shock, Kola realised that there was a face among the enemy that he recognised. The features were long and thin, the mouth cruel and downturned, the eyes black with bitterness beneath a wolfskin helmet.

Matotope! Kola couldn't believe his eyes until the treacherous shaman leaned in towards him and whispered cruel words above the beat of horses' hooves.

'You think you are strong, Four Winds,' he snarled. 'But let us see now how the boy stands up in battle!'

Kola struck out in anger with his knife. He caught the blade in the mane of Matotope's horse and felt himself wrenched from Silver Cloud's back.

Meanwhile, Snake Eye himself had charged ahead and rounded on Silver Cloud, who, free of his rider, raised himself high on his hind legs and pawed the air.

Silver Cloud's hooves smashed down close to the Chief's head. Snake Eye ducked to avoid them, clinging to the side of his black-and-white mare. From under her belly, he reached out and swiped the blade of his tomahawk down Silver Cloud's side.

As Kola rolled clear of other horses' thundering hooves, he heard Silver Cloud scream in pain and twist away from Snake Eye, only to clash with Matotope. Now the dream horse was hemmed in and bleeding from his side.

He fell to his knees then struggled up again. With a stagger he turned to fetch Kola, but Snake Eye blocked his way. Blood streamed from Silver Cloud's wound and stained the ground. Kola darted towards him but was flung aside by the charging fury of another Wild Dog horse. Then he watched in horror as two of the men threw ropes which circled around Silver Cloud's neck. They drew the lassos tight. Silver Cloud fought back, twisting and writhing to be free. But the ropes strangled him and stole his breath.

Then Snake Eye cried out a command and led his small band down the gulley. His men surrounded Silver

Cloud and dragged him after their leader, letting out triumphant yells. Last of all, Matotope circled his horse on the spot where the dream horse's blood stained the ground. He raised his knife to the sky in cruel exultation.

'Return to Red Hawk and tell him that his sun is truly set!' he cried to Four Winds. 'The quest is ended, and his People shall die!'

FOUR

Kola tasted the bitterness of defeat.

All the hopes of the White Water Sioux had rested with him, and now they were dashed to the ground where Silver Cloud's blood seeped into the sand. What was left but for the boy to return to the mountains and tell how he had failed?

He stood alone in the valley where his hopes had died, bleeding a little from a cut on his arm and wishing for death.

For a while he sat in the dirt. The sound of hooves had faded, but Matotope's last words still rang in his ears. The sun beat down on him, a small, solitary figure sitting slumped in the dirt.

Though Kola's body was still, his thoughts whirled. Ahead lay an impossible journey into the deepest mine, guarded by monsters, protected by the fearful Unktehi. But behind lay defeat and the deaths of all his band.

He saw the faces of the warriors, One Horn and the rest, and recalled the battles they had fought. Then there were the children: three boys of his own age, the girls and the small ones. The women would weep over them and bewail their fates.

Most of all Kola thought of Red Hawk and White Deer waiting by their tipi, watching as he climbed the mountain alone. Their old hearts would feel the stab of pain when they realised he had returned without the diamond. And was this the way that he, Four Winds, should repay them for the blessing of life?

No, he would go on, he decided. Snake Eye and Matotope believed that he was too weak to face the bad spirits of Yellow Water alone, and perhaps he was. But Kola knew that one did not always need to be strong to defeat the enemy. He could call instead upon the trickery of Coyote and the wisdom of Raven to outsmart Unktehi. If he kept his wits about him, then he might still succeed.

But meanwhile he grew weak. The sun was draining his strength and he was losing blood from the cut on his arm. So, seeking out the shade of the nearest rock, he untied his medicine bundle, the gift from his grandfather, and laid the contents on the ground.

First he took up a necklace of turquoise beads from which hung an eagle's feather. Putting this around his neck, he knew he would run faster than ever before. Then he opened a small bag of herbs, took out the dry, strong-smelling powder and rubbed it into his wound. The cut burned like fire, then the pain died away. Kola retied the pouch and returned it to his medicine bundle.

'May the power of this bundle be great,' he muttered, rolling up the contents and slinging the pack across his shoulder.

He began a chant as he walked back into the sun.

> *'Sumka ismala*
> *miyelo ca*
> *maka oka winhya*
> *oma wani.'*

I am lone wolf, I roam in different places. The sight of a lizard watching him from the rock where he had

147

sheltered put him in good heart, for after all, it was as his grandmother had said: Lizard brings long life.

Kola walked on through the valley. He grieved as he went for the loss of Silver Cloud, his friend. The beautiful creature had been cut down, ropes choking him, and the dust had risen into a dark cloud as Snake Eye, his warriors and the treacherous Matotope had dragged him away.

The sight of the disgraced shaman flashed before the boy's eyes. He had snarled like a wolf from under his helmet, his black eyes glittering as he held his lightning knife to the sky and sent his own People into oblivion.

Soon, if Matotope had his way, there would be none left of the White Water Sioux. Their bones would become dust and sweep from the mountains into the valleys of their homelands. Their dead voices would call in the wind.

'Four Winds, wait for me!' a girl's voice cried from the jagged horizon.

At first Kola mistook it for the wailing of his People when they learned their fate. He walked on solemnly without looking up.

'Four Winds!' Hidden Moon called again. Hot sand blew up from the deep valley and stung her bare legs and arms. For two nights and almost two days she had trailed her friend and his dream horse. Often she had lost their tracks and had to speak with the birds of the air and the creatures of the plains and the hot mountains to discover where the travellers were headed. She talked to the grazing buffalo and to the wheeling crows, and they had taken her the way she needed to go.

Seeing that he did not answer, she left the ridge and dipped into the valley, her feet sliding over the loose earth, which sent larger stones peppering down the hill. Soon her descent had set up a small landslide which Kola couldn't help but notice.

He shaded his eyes and looked up into the sun. Was this friend or enemy?

Hidden Moon slid and scrambled down the slope, reaching for handholds in the rock. From her vantage point on the ridge she'd seen Snake Eye and his riders sweep into the valley and capture Silver Cloud. With a shock she'd recognised the wolfskin helmet and cloak of Matotope.

'Wait for me. I will join you. Together we will find the diamond!' she promised.

Kola knew her voice first. The she stepped into the shadow and he could make out her figure. Smaller, more slender than he was, younger still. 'Go back!' he told her angrily. 'This is no place for children!'

The girl ran to his side. 'I will not return. I will go with you to find the precious stone!'

He stopped in his tracks. 'This is foolish. You are my cousin, the granddaughter of my grandfather's brother. I will not let you give up your life.'

Prepared for this answer, Hidden Moon stood in his path. 'I have told you that I did not trust Matotope, and left the village and travelled alone by night. I have swum rivers and braved the buffalo. I saw you almost killed by fire and the great gift of rain that came with the rainbow. I do not stand here now, your equal, only to be told to return to my tipi.'

'Why did you come?' he demanded.

'For the same reason as you.' She stood defiantly in front of him. 'Because I cannot stay in the village and wait for Snake Eye to drive us out.'

'But I went on my dream quest to Spider Rock,' he reminded her. 'Only then did they permit me to make this journey.'

'I am a girl. They would not send me to seek a vision. That is how it is.' Hidden Moon held her head up. 'I came in any case.'

Kola puzzled over what to do. Should he tell his

proud cousin that her help was not welcome, or should he accept it? Back in the village, the women would worry over Hidden Moon's absence. They would fear that a mountain lion or bear had stolen down from the mountain and taken her. There would be much weeping. On the other hand, he recalled her anger at being made to live a life in the tipi and by the cooking pot, where she would weave baskets and sew beads on to war shirts until she was old.

'I am sad about Silver Cloud,' Hidden Moon told Kola. 'I quickly learned to love him when I guarded him by the cedar tree.'

'Did you see where Snake Eye took him?' Kola asked sharply. He thought that perhaps she had seen more from high on the hill.

But she shook her head. 'They vanished into another gulley. The horse fought them but he could not break free.' She glanced at Four Winds' pale face and bloodstained arm. 'Are you weak from the wound?'

'A little,' he confessed.

So Hidden Moon drew an object from the beaded pouch she wore around her waist. It was a long, white plaited band, woven in with small silver discs. 'Wear this around your wrist,' she told Four Winds. 'Silver Cloud bade me take hairs from his mane and weave it into an amulet to protect anyone who wears it.'

Kola grunted and held out his wrist. He imagined the power that the silken, silvery band would bring.

'Let us go,' she murmured, as if it was useless for him to argue further.

He looked into her determined, dark eyes. Here was his match. 'Yes', he conceded, 'let us go.'

Snake Eye, Matotope and the rest took Silver Cloud back to where the main band waited in the baking hot desert.

A hundred Comanche warriors got to their feet and raised their voices in praise of Anteep of the underworld. 'Oh, Great Spirit be praised that he has delivered this gift of the dream horse to us! May our enemies perish. May the Wild Dogs flourish!'

Their chief dragged the prisoner into their midst. Silver Cloud's coat was dull with the red dust of the desert, there was dried blood down his side. He did not resist as men threw more ropes around his neck and legs until he was tied fast and unable to move.

Then Snake Eye called for the War Bundle to be brought from the Tent of War. He took out the skins of birds and held them up in the still air and appealed to the war gods to bring them victory. 'For the swallow and the hawk are messengers of war!' he cried. 'And we invoke their power!'

His warriors chanted in support, gathering around Silver Cloud in a tight circle several men deep.

Then Matotope took off his wolfskin headdress and handed it with much ceremony to Snake Eye. 'The life of the warrior is like that of a wolf!' he cried. 'We lie in wait, we prowl through the bush, we pounce! I give this sacred robe and my spirit powers to you, my new chief, that you may succeed in battle against my sworn enemy, the White Water Sioux!'

Snake Eye took the robe and placed it around his shoulders. His men began a dance of war, creeping low and springing forward like the wolf they worshipped.

At the centre of the circle Silver Cloud stood hobbled. He gazed out over the men's heads, across the desert into a shimmering heat haze. The pinnacles on the horizon quivered, the sun was blood red.

'Death to the spirit horse!' the Wild Dogs yelled. 'He bears the enemy on his back and is sent by Ghost Horse to punish us!'

Silver Cloud saw the men take up their spears wrapped with otter skins and trailing eagle feathers. They held them aloft, crying for his blood. He was saddened at the spectacle.

153

Snake Eye stood apart with Matotope. His heart beat coldly and slowly as he raised his right hand, its palm towards the heavens. 'Kill the dream horse!' he ordered.

The Wild Dogs aimed their spears.

At a certain moment, as Four Winds and Hidden Moon left the steep canyon and came into a wider valley where trees grew and some buffalo grazed, the boy felt a strange breath of wind across his face. It cooled and soothed him, and brought with it a whispering voice.

'Wisdom and courage, strength and speed. I bring all these!'

Four Winds looked around to find that the voice had tricked him, for there was no one nearby.

'Above all, I bring you loyalty,' the spirit voice murmured.

'What is it?' Hidden Moon asked Four Winds. She saw that he was transfixed by something which she could not see or hear.

'Silver Cloud is present,' he warned. If no longer in body, then still in spirit.

'I bring you loyalty. I will never fail you. Love sits in my heart.'

The boy walked on thankfully, the girl at his side.

154

*　*　*

As the second day of his journey ended and the sun faded into the west, a Raven came to talk with them.

'Where are you travelling to?' The bird had alighted on a stricken tree, made bare and twisted by a lightning strike. He had watched them approach, his shiny black head cocked to one side. Then he had spoken in a cheerful voice.

'To Yellow Water,' Four Winds replied. 'To find a diamond in the deepest mine.'

'Alone?' the bird asked in some surprise.

'Why not?' The boy tried to sound confident, but his body shook. He knew the raven as the wisest of birds and so feared his advice. 'Can you tell us: are we walking in the right direction?'

The bird nodded. 'You are almost there. Tomorrow, when the sun rises, the giant canyon will appear and the lake will spread before your eyes. To the east of Yellow Water lies the mine you speak of.'

Four Winds thanked him, then made as if to hurry on.

'Unktehi's monsters guard the entrance,' the raven said, slowly flapping his wings and rising from the blackened branch. He flew lazily above their heads. 'They are many and dangerous.'

155

'Do they know we are coming?' Hidden Moon asked. She too was nervous of the raven.

'They know everything,' he replied. 'And remember, no one has ever passed through the entrance, though many have tried.'

Four Winds frowned and quickened his pace.

The raven floated on an airstream to their right. 'Unktehi himself resides there. Only the foolish dare approach.'

Or those with the cleverness of the coyote, Four Winds thought to himself.

'And can we be certain that this is the entrance to the deepest mine in the world?' Hidden Moon asked.

'You can be sure of that,' the raven cawed. 'Just as there are diamonds in the ground. But you must travel far with the earth above your heads to find them. I hear from the chipmunk and mole that sometimes rocks fall and block the tunnels. If you do outsmart Unktehi and his guards and enter the mine, then you must take great care that the roof doesn't fall on you.'

Hidden Moon shuddered. But then she remembered the bracelet of hair which she had made for Four Winds. 'We draw our strength from Ghost Horse,' she told the raven bravely. 'He sent his spirit, Silver Cloud, to protect Four Winds. The roof will not fall!'

'But Ghost Horse has allowed his messenger to be taken and tortured by your enemy,' the bird pointed out, wheeling slowly around. It seemed that he'd almost finished what he had come to say. 'I have a vision of Silver Cloud staked to the earth, facing a hundred sharp spears.'

'Stop!' Kola begged. 'I don't want to know!'

'Would Silver Cloud wish you to continue this way?' The raven's last remark was designed to leave the boy and girl in grave doubt. Slowly he flapped his ragged wings.

The question brought Kola to a standstill. He stared ahead, towards the south and the canyon that split the world in two.

A breath of wind spoke. '*I will never fail you. Love sits in my heart.*'

'Yes, he would wish us to continue,' he told the raven. 'Tomorrow we will go to Yellow Water, come what may.'

FIVE

Four Winds and Hidden
Moon walked through the
night towards the Yellow
Water Canyon. The stars
guided them and the light
of the moon showed them
where to put their feet.

They shared their
journey with the mountain
lion and coyote who stalked
through the bush and crept
along moonlit ridges. Once
or twice they heard the
sudden snap of twigs and
the rustle of leaves, the high
cry of a helpless victim
drowned by a loud snarl
and a snap. In the silence
that followed, life ebbed
and a meal was made.

The sound of the hunt made the travellers' flesh creep. They could picture the glistening white fangs of the coyote and the bright yellow eyes of the lion. Worse still, Hidden Moon spotted an owl circling above them, a soft prophet of doom.

'Look!' She held Four Winds by the arm and pointed to the pale shape floating in a current of air.

The owl circled, tilting its broad wings to catch another breath of wind, wheeling high above their heads.

It was an ill omen – but Four Winds put the vision to one side. He did not want to speak with the owl, for nothing was going to prevent him reaching the canyon and the entrance to the mine.

Before dawn they entered the place which split the world in two. There were many valleys cut by a turbulent river, sided by sheer cliffs rising high into the sky. It was as if the water had smashed its way through mountain after mountain, wearing away the yellow rock, finally finding its bed on harder, darker granite deep in the earth's crust.

Kola saw this in the grey dawn and was overcome by the splendour of the canyon. He wondered how water could cut through rock and how the wind and rain could wear away the mountains. He felt small and humble, and far away from his homeland.

Hidden Moon too realised that they had almost reached the end of their journey. She followed the route of the wild white water, searching for the place where the river ran into the lake, Yellow Water. But a mist rose from the mighty river and curled around the base of the canyon, drifting up the rugged sides until the sun appeared at the rim of the highest ridge. There, where the golden pink rays met the white mist, was an explosion of rainbow colours, which gladdened her and gave her the heart to go on.

As the sun rose, Four Winds and Hidden Moon stopped to drink. The water from the mighty river was cool in their dry mouths. They let it trickle through their fingers, scooped again and splashed it on to their tired faces. Then they looked up at the sun and took courage from the dawning of a new day.

They hadn't walked on more than a hundred paces from their watering place when a sound and a movement from a shallow cave on the opposite bank caught their attention. A weak human cry rose above the swirl and lap of the water against the banks.

Startled, Four Winds scrambled on to a high rock and peered across. He made out the figure of a girl crouching inside the entrance to the cave, her hands

161

stretched out as if pleading for rescue. She was young – perhaps seven or eight summers – with her long hair coiled strangely around her head, and wearing a woven shawl and skirt of deep sky blue.

'Who is there?' Hidden Moon asked, climbing on to the rock. She gasped when she saw the solitary child.

'We must go and speak with her,' Four Winds decided.

'How? By swimming across this great river?' Hidden Moon held back. 'There could be danger in the water.' Monsters like Yietso who ate human flesh and Tehotsodi who could flood the whole world. 'And what if the girl is a vision created by evil spirits to trick us?'

Four Winds knew this was possible. 'You think that Unktehi and his master, Anteep, know that we approach the mine?' he asked.

Hidden Moon nodded. 'Raven told us so.' She stared at the girl crouching in the cave. 'This is an evil vision,' she insisted. 'We must ignore her and go on our way.'

But the boy was not certain. The child looked ill, as if a fever had raged through her small body. It seemed that she couldn't stand or even crawl out of the cave towards the water's edge. 'We can't pass her by,' he insisted. 'Let me swim across and speak with her.'

Hidden Moon sighed. Time was precious. 'Then do it quickly,' she urged, still afraid that the child was other than she seemed.

So Four Winds took off his medicine bundle, but kept the feather necklace and band of silver horsehair around his neck and wrist. As he prepared to dive into the yellow water, he touched the lizardskin pouch on his belt. Then he threw himself head first into the river.

He plunged underwater and gave a strong kick. The river was deep and the current powerful. He had to swim against it so as not to be dragged too far downriver. After two more strokes through the murky depths, he pushed for the surface.

Hidden Moon waited anxiously for Four Winds' head to break clear of the surface. Her heart beat fast and uneven. She was sure that Yietso was down there on the muddy bed, gloating over the trick he had played.

But then her cousin appeared, his black hair smooth as an otter's against his skull, swimming hard for the opposite bank. The child cried louder as rescue approached.

Four Winds fought the current to stay even with the cave. He felt it tug at his legs to slow him down and drag him back towards the river bed, so he kicked harder than ever, using his arms to pull him towards the bank.

At last he made it and hauled himself out of the water. Now he could hear the girl sobbing and pleading for help, still crouched inside the dark cave. So, with water streaming from him, he climbed up beside her.

'Don't be afraid,' he said softly.

Now that he had arrived, the girl cowered back into the cave, which was low and dark. This was no evil spirit who had shape-shifted into a helpess child, he decided, for these were real tears she was weeping.

Four Winds waited for her to grow less afraid, then said, 'Tell me your name.'

'Gilspa,' she answered, shaking with fear. 'I am a child of the Tesaktumo People of the Hopi nation. Our home was Kooyama.'

The boy recognised with a start the name of the cave village through which he and Silver Cloud had passed. He recalled the carved doorways and empty steps. 'What happened to your people?' he asked.

'We left our homeland when the spirits took away our water,' she explained. 'Our Chief Hatali died of a fever and our People were scattered.'

Four Winds listened with sorrow. 'Tell me how you came to be here.'

'My mother hid me in this cave when the Comanche war party came amongst us,' Gilspa explained. 'There were a hundred spears and many women and children died.'

'Where were your warriors?'

'Gone to fish in the Yellow River and to hunt buffalo on the plain. Snake Eye chose his time well.'

Anger rose in Four Winds' throat. His hatred for Snake Eye grew stronger than ever. 'What happened to your mother?'

'She hid me here and promised to return. I grew hungry, my hands shake, I am afraid.'

'I know Snake Eye and his Wild Dogs,' Four Winds said bitterly. 'He is sworn enemy of my people, the White Water Sioux. He slew my father and took my mother.'

'Then you will help me?' Gilspa begged. Her round, dark eyes were full of tears, her small mouth trembled.

He nodded. 'I will take you across the river and search for what is left of your People, the Tesaktumos. We will not part until I have found your cousins.'

She wept now for gladness, climbing on to Four Winds' back and clasping her hands tight around his neck. He climbed down from the cave and entered the river slowly, keeping above the surface and swimming steadily to the shore where Hidden Moon waited.

'We must go back to Kooyama,' he told his cousin. 'Gilspa is sick. She needs to be with her People, the Tesaktumo Hopis.

The news made Hidden Moon frown deeply. 'We cannot go back to that place,' she protested. 'The village is empty. What would we gain?'

Four Winds knew that Hidden Moon could not bear any delay in their quest for the diamond. 'I know, it is difficult,' he admitted, setting the girl gently on the bank. 'But I cannot leave her here.'

'Why not? Is not the future of the White Water People more important than the life of one small Hopi girl?' Hidden Moon argued. 'Why must you delay by returning to Kooyama?'

'Because it is not in my heart to let her die. She is sick and helpless. She has wept enough.'

Hidden Moon's voice rose. 'Then you are a fool!' she cried. 'You have been tricked by a spirit who has taken the shape of a pretty girl. Unktehi is cunning. He knows how to divert you from your quest now that Silver Cloud is not here to guide you!'

Four Winds took a deep breath. 'I do not think this is Unktehi's work.' He looked again at the girl who shook and wept all the more as the two cousins argued.

'I must take her back to her People.'

'This is not flesh and blood!' Hidden Moon shouted. She flung open Four Winds' medicine bundle and delved into the pouch containing herbs.

Gilspa shied away, back against a rock.

'See, she shrinks from your medicine as though from poison. Only an evil spirit from the underworld refuses to be made better, knowing that to take the medicine will change him back into the evil monster that he is!'

'Stop. Do not frighten her.' Four Winds came between Hidden Moon and Gilspa. 'I have made up my mind to do what my grandmother, White Deer, has taught me. I must cast away self-interest and look and listen for the welfare of others.'

He spoke calmly. Hidden Moon knew that she had lost the argument. 'My cousin,' she said in a broken voice. 'Kola!'

'Will you come with us?' he asked, taking Gilspa on his back once more.

Hidden Moon shook her head. 'I will go forward.'

'Then stay by the river until you reach Yellow Water,' he instructed. 'The canyon will be broad and deep. Wait there by the lake until I return.'

'I will do all I can to seek the mine,' she insisted.

'But you will not enter alone.' Four Winds was afraid

for her now. 'Remember, it is I who must fetch the diamond, as Ghost Horse ordered. If we are to save our People, it must be me.'

Reluctantly Hidden Moon bowed her head in agreement. 'Your heart is kind and true,' she told him sadly.

It was hard for Four Winds to turn away from the cousin he loved, for she walked alone into danger. But he found her headstrong. He thought she lacked judgement and kindness towards the Hopi girl. '*Maka akanl wicasa iyuha el.*' Go in peace, he told her.

'So with you,' she replied, making one last silent appeal with her eyes.

He turned away with the burden of the child. Gilspa's arms almost choked him as they set off back towards Kooyama. She weighed more than he'd imagined and his steps were slow.

'Where did your people go after they were driven from the cave village?' he asked. The sides of the great canyon closed in on him as they re-entered the smaller gulleys of the night before. The coyotes and the lions kept watch once more.

'They fled far,' Gilspa replied. 'When Chief Hatali died and Snake Eye attacked, they were driven into the dry hills, away from the water. I do not know where they are now.'

'And your mother. After she hid you in the cave, where did she go?'

The child on his back wept. 'She went away, who knows where. Perhaps the Wild Dogs caught her and put her to death.'

'They also took my mother, Shining Star,' he confided. His heart had broken in two and never mended. He knew how Gilspa must feel.

After many paces, as the sun reached its height, Four Winds tired. He stopped by a creek and eased the child from his back. She sighed and moaned and said her whole body shook with fever.

'You must drink,' he told her, showing her a way down the steep bank of the stream. 'If your head is hot with fever, then you must bathe it in the cool stream.'

But she held back and refused to take his hand. 'I cannot walk,' she whimpered.

So he went alone and drank, then held his palms together and filled them so that he would have water to take to the child. She lay on her side on the ground as if sleeping, her back turned, her black hair coiled in a strange, snake-like design over her head. The water trickled slowly through Four Winds' fingers as he bent over her.

A drop landed on her woven shawl and sank through, another on her blue skirt. There was little left in his hands as he sprinkled it on the girl's hair and face to cool her fever.

The water splashed. The figure on the ground writhed and coiled, rearing up as a giant serpent, high above Four Winds' head.

Four Winds staggered back. He gazed up at the snake's flat, scaly black head and soft yellow throat. It had eyes like emeralds with a slash of black pupil; its thin, forked tongue flickered towards him.

The snake laughed as Four Winds drew his knife. 'This is the boy who comes to steal a diamond from the deepest mine!' he cried. 'Poor fool; he is easier to trick than a newborn baby. What chance then of outwitting Unktehi and taking the stone back to save his People?'

And Four Winds cursed and cried out against his own childish simplicity. He swiped with his knife at the serpent, who slid beyond reach, his black scales glistening. 'Kill me, then!' he yelled, sick of being the plaything of the cruel spirits. 'Crush me to death, poison me with your tongue!'

The snake dipped its head and began to coil its body around the boy.

Four Winds felt his arms being pinned against his side, felt the pressure of the snake's body against his ribs. He did not resist. *Forgive me*, he prayed to Red Hawk, his grandfather. And to all the others among his People whose futures he had destroyed.

SIX

The canyon walls rose to meet the sun. They were immense, bare cliffs which dwarfed all objects and made the mighty Yellow River which ran through the yawning gap seem like a slow trickle.

Hidden Moon held her breath as she entered the canyon. It was as they said: this crack in the rock could split the world in two. Sighing deeply, she went forward, a tiny, fearful figure in the hot, deserted landscape.

The sun beat down. There was no wind. Hidden Moon ventured on in a

storm of fear, anger and confusion.

Four Winds had been drawn away from his quest to save his People because of the kindness in his heart. Hidden Moon saw danger in his rescue of the girl, Gilspa. On the other hand, she recognised that the child, if she *was* who she claimed to be, was, like them, a helpless victim of evil spirits and Snake Eye's band. But her cousin's tender-hearted action had left her alone in the desert to continue the search for the diamond. That could not be right.

'He is foolish!' she cried out loud to the birds high above and the water rushing by her feet. 'If he must save Gilspa, why doesn't he bring the girl with us on our journey, and afterwards take her to find her People?'

She was sick, she could not walk, came the answer.

'I do not believe that,' Hidden Moon said aloud.

That is because you are hard-hearted.

'She would not take medicine for her fever.'

Children are afraid of medicine. Gilspa had been alone in the cave for two nights, praying for her mother to return. Her fear was great.

'Mine also,' Hidden Moon sighed. She gazed ahead to where the rushing river widened and curved across the flat bottom of the canyon, eventually flowing into the largest lake she had ever seen.

The sight of Yellow Water slowed her pace. There was her journey's end, there lay the diamond that would save her People. And yet she felt fear rise within her. Four Winds had gone. The dream horse was no more. She must face Unktehi alone.

Raven saw the girl stop by the edge of the lake. He picked her out as he wheeled over the canyon, knew that she was alone and afraid.

So he flapped his wings and sailed on an air current close to the ground, alighting on a smooth rock close to where Hidden Moon stood. He hopped to a place where she could easily see him, settled his feathers and spoke.

'Where is the boy you were travelling with?'

'Gone,' Hidden Moon muttered.

'And left you alone?' the bird cawed. 'What was he thinking of?'

'You must find him and ask him yourself,' she replied angrily, 'for I have no idea why Four Winds put the Hopi girl before the future of the White Water People.'

'Hmm.' Raven ducked his glossy head. 'Tell me more.'

So Hidden Moon described the girl in the cave and her cousin's brave rescue. 'Now he carries her back to

Kooyama in search of her People,' she reported, noticing that the bird grew agitated as she spoke.

'This Hopi girl – she was small, with her hair wound about her head, and wearing a coloured shawl?' he asked.

Hidden Moon nodded fearfully. 'Her name is Gilspa.'

'This is not her name!' Raven announced. 'Neither is she from the village of Kooyama. In truth, this is Yietso, dread monster who guards the mine with Unktehi. He takes many shapes to fool his enemies, and one of these is the girl, Gilspa!'

The news made Hidden Moon cry out. 'In my heart I knew!'

'You are wise,' Raven commented. He admired the girl and wished to give her advice that would save her own life. 'Know then that it is dangerous for you to continue alone, without the guidance of Ghost Horse's messenger, Silver Cloud, and without the help of the boy, Four Winds.'

Hidden Moon nodded. Tears sprang to her eyes as she imagined Four Winds' fate at the hands of Yietso, the flesh-eater.

'Then you will give up this quest,' Raven insisted.

'I cannot!' she cried. 'While there is a chance that I

might find the diamond and take it back to my People, I must go on!'

'But this is only the first of three quests,' Raven reminded her. 'The task is too great. Go home and tell your Chief Red Hawk that it is impossible.'

'I cannot!' she said again, shaking her head while the tears fell.

Raven regarded her sadly. 'You have a brave heart,' he told her. 'You would not sit waiting in the tipi, but came after your cousin and the dream horse.'

'Why must I sit and wait because I am a girl?' she cried. 'I have as much courage as a boy, my brain is quick and my body is strong.'

The bird continued to gaze at her with his bright, black eyes. 'Go home,' he repeated, more quietly than before. 'Follow my advice before it is too late.'

But Hidden Moon dried her tears. 'I will go forward,' she decided. 'And what will be will be.'

The shadowy rocks were still cool in the morning sun when Hidden Moon came to the entrance to the mine. It lay on the eastern shore of the vast lake whose water was an intense blue under a clear sky. She studied the opening carefully. It was the height of two men, but the width was narrow. A ledge of yellow rock overhung the opening, casting a dark shadow.

The girl stood in the sun, gazing all around. The surface of the lake rippled under a hot breeze. In the distance, a small herd of antelope stopped to drink before they hurried on down the bare canyon to good grazing land beyond.

Taking in the peaceful scene, her sore heart eased. Instead of the monsters she had been warned about, there was calm and beauty beneath a pure blue sky.

Soaring high, Raven looked down sadly.

Perhaps she had caught Unktehi offguard, Hidden Moon thought. The dreaded guardian of the mine had not been expecting her and had used all his energies to help the Wild Dogs trap Silver Cloud and send Yietso to cheat Four Winds. Now he was sleeping.

And so it was possible for Hidden Moon to creep unnoticed into the tunnel that lay beyond the quiet entrance. She entered the shadow of the overhang and peered inside, waiting for her eyes to grow accustomed to the darkness.

A small lizard ran clear of the tunnel, its pale, thin body passing close by the girl's feet.

Hidden Moon braced herself and stepped inside. The sudden cold hit her and made her shiver. A silence deeper than she had ever known enfolded her. She gritted her teeth and made herself go forward.

Darkness pressed in on her. She breathed in its dampness, smelt decay all around. Feeling for the walls of the tunnel, she discovered that they were rough and close together, though the roof was still higher than she could reach.

I am surrounded by rock, she thought. *It is above my head and beneath my feet.*

And then Unktehi, who had been silently watching all this while, acted. He laughed to himself at how easy it was to defeat these puny enemies. What need was there of a storm and a great disturbance of nature when a mere loosening of rocks above the girl's head would be enough?

Hidden Moon could see nothing, but she heard a stone dislodge and fall at her feet. Dust sprinkled on to her face, then another stone fell. The roof of the tunnel was cracking.

Fear gripped her heart. She turned back, only to find that stones were loosening and dropping on all sides. She stumbled on one, turned again and again until she lost all sense of which way to run. And now the dust came down like rain and choked her, the rocks overhead grating and shifting with a huge, grinding shudder.

Hidden Moon tried to run, but falling rocks prevented her. She gasped and went down on her hands and knees, scrambling back towards what she thought was the entrance. There was dirt in her mouth; stones bruised her as they dropped. A light glowed a little way ahead. She was sure it was the sun and she struggled past larger rocks and boulders that blocked the way.

Unktehi smiled again. Then he released a final shower of rocks.

It is not yet time!' Yietso declared with a cruel smile as he loosened Four Winds from his coiled grip.

The boy fell to the ground, dazed and breathless. He gazed in bewilderment at the giant black serpent rearing over him.

'Go!' Yietso hissed. 'Unktehi has said that you must live!'

Four Winds groaned at the aching of his ribs. The monster had curled around him, intent on crushing him to death. And yet, suddenly, as the darkness began to close in on him and the world swam from his grasp, the snake had released him.

Yietso stared down with cold, cruel eyes. He was growing larger, filling the narrow gulley where the stream ran its course. As he increased in size, his black scales grew indistinct, as if melting into a cloud hovering above the boy. Yet his emerald eyes remained clear.

'I don't understand!' Four Winds gasped. 'Why not kill me now?'

'Because your time has not come,' the monster sneered. 'Unktehi has spoken.'

Four Winds rose from the ground, taking up his medicine bundle and bear club knife. He was weary, his heart sickened by the shape-shifting spirit. With an angry gesture of defiance, he raised his knife. 'I will not give in!' he declared. 'While there is breath in my body I will search for the diamond!'

Yietso melted into a dark cloud, his green eyes flickering. 'You give us good sport,' he mocked. 'One boy alone against the might of Unktehi!'

One boy and one girl! Four Winds remembered that Hidden Moon was by Yellow Water, waiting by the deepest mine.

There was laughter in the sky as the cloud dissolved into the air.

The thought of his cousin sent Four Winds running back through the narrow gulleys and across streams that led in time to the great canyon and Yellow Water. He forgot the weariness of his legs and the aching of his ribs, ignoring the signs in the landscape that would have told him that Hidden Moon had passed by. So he leapt creeks and overlooked footprints, then ran by the cave where he had foolishly stopped to rescue Gilspa. For Hidden Moon had sworn that she would go forward, and there was proud stubbornness in her heart.

As a child of four summers she had said to him, 'Teach me to hunt.' At six she had learned to fashion a bow of hickory, at seven she had brought back rabbits and a small deer. Now she had proved herself his equal by travelling alone in the footsteps of Silver Cloud.

Four Winds had told Hidden Moon to wait by the lake until he returned, but he could not be sure that she would heed his advice. Her eyes had begged him not to take the girl to Kooyama, but he had refused. Why then should she wait as he had asked?

Fear for his cousin and the eagle's feather which he wore around his neck gave speed to the boy's feet. He should have given her the silver horsehair band to keep her safe, he thought now. As it was, she had gone unguarded.

Shortly after the sun had reached its height, Four Winds entered the canyon of Yellow Water. His feet caused a thin trail of dust to rise as he made for the eastern shore and sought the entrance to the deepest mine.

'Hidden Moon!' he called. His voice drifted against the sides of the canyon and came back as the faintest of echoes. 'Hidden Moon, I am sorry! You were right about the Hopi girl!'

The water in the lake rippled and sparkled as it had done when she had passed by. Far above, the Raven watched.

The eastern shore was made of soft sand sloping gently to the water's edge. Four Winds easily picked out Hidden Moon's footprints, which he followed as far as a cave with an overhanging rock shading its entrance. Here the trail stopped.

'Hidden Moon!' he shouted, cursing the dull echo which tricked him into thinking that she had replied. He closed his eyes and groaned when he saw that she had entered the mine alone.

No! he told himself. *She would not! This is another of Unktehi's tricks to lure me inside to my death!* He spun round, expecting to see Yietso laughing behind his back, or the dreaded guardian of the mine himself, taking a monstrous shape. But no; there were only faint clouds on the horizon, rolling into the canyon and screening the high sun behind a white haze.

183

A wind fluttered through the long fringes of Four Winds' war shirt as he turned to look once more at the tall, dark entrance to the mine. There was a gloomy feel about it, with the overhanging ledge, and the air inside seemed thick with dust. As the boy looked and listened, he heard small rocks fall from the roof and rattle to the ground.

They fell with a dull, light echo and made the startled observer's eyes open wide. He went forward jerkily towards the entrance, then stepped over stones that had rolled clear of the mine and now blocked his path.

'Hidden Moon!' he whispered.

He picked his way into the tunnel. Hope flared when he tried to tell himself that the rockfall had been slight. These rocks were not big, and surely the roof was strong.

But though the dust still swirled, he could see that the tunnel ahead was blocked. Shielding his eyes with his hand, he crouched low and stared into the gloom.

Three paces ahead, Hidden Moon lay on the ground as if sleeping. Her eyes were closed, her cheek resting against the cold rock.

Four Winds crept towards her. He brushed the dirt from her face and leaned close. There was no breath. Her spirit had passed.

So he lifted the rocks from her body and carried her out of the mine into the sunlight. He laid her by the shore of the lake, then sat by her side. She was pale and cold as he unbraided her long hair and spread it about her shoulders.

'*Iki 'cize waon 'kon.*' It is over, he whispered.

His heart ached, but he did not cry.

SEVEN

Four Winds buried his cousin, Hidden Moon, on the shore of Yellow Water. He knew that she must cross the mountains and return to their White Water homeland on her way to the land of the dead.

'Behold!' he cried to the heavens. 'May her spirit rise to the stars and travel peacefully into the hereafter!'

Then he took his knife and scratched the shape of a mighty Thunder Bird into the smooth rock close to where he had buried her. The bird, Wakinyan, had wide, flapping wings.

He brought thunder and lightning which the travelling spirit might harness to clear obstacles out of her way.

In his heart Four Winds grieved for his cousin, but still his eyes remained dry.

Hidden Moon had followed the way of *Cante Tinz*, the Strong Hearts. She had not been a coward and run from danger. Instead, she had found the courage to go forward alone into the mine. Four Winds honoured her and chanted as he withdrew from her grave. 'He who turns away shall not be admitted.'

As he looked towards the dark entrance, he was aware of clouds gathering. Thunder Bird was getting ready to flap his wings to assist Hidden Moon on her journey. Four Winds heard the low rumble in the sky and was satisfied.

But as he left the grave and walked towards the mine, the rumble grew to a roar which rolled through the bruised sky, then echoed as an ear-splitting crack directly overhead. Instead of preparing to guide the spirit of Hidden Moon on her way, it seemed that the Thunder Bird was angry and about to unleash a cruel storm into the dusty canyon.

Sure enough, the crash of thunder was soon followed by a flash of lightning which ripped the sky apart. It shot to earth, its forked path reflected in the lake, sending a shock wave that would paralyse all who saw it.

Four Winds felt a huge dread pass through him. Already plunged deep in grief by the loss of Silver Cloud and Hidden Moon, the ill omen of the approaching storm almost made him sink to the ground.

All is against me. The world is my enemy, and I must fight Unktehi alone! he cried to himself.

Overhead, a second flash of silver lightning tore the sky.

Then the rain began. It fell as slow, cold drops on Four Winds' upturned face. Then it came down faster, heavier, until, blown by a fierce wind, it lashed his skin and blurred his vision. The cold force of it made him seek shelter under a ledge of rock, staggering there across sandy soil which was already criss-crossed with muddy channels made by the downpour. Eventually he found refuge and huddled against the rock.

Four Winds took a deep breath. He must prepare himself to enter the mine and risk everything to find the diamond. The stone was deep underground, at the end of many dark tunnels, protected by Unktehi and his evil spirits.

Perhaps this storm was the work of Unktehi's

demons, who had gathered the forces of nature to fling them against Four Winds' first attempt to enter the mine. As a child he had learned of the monster, Tehotsodi, who came armed with floods to drown his enemies.

Yes, Four Winds thought to himself, *Tehotsodi will send a wall of water into the mine so that no man will reach the diamond!*

Or else, Yietso has returned to his master, Unktehi, and this is another of their games to frighten me and send me running back to my People!

Soaked to the skin, his grandfather's war shirt dripping and clinging to his skinny body, Four Winds stared out into the raging storm.

Then, in a roll of thunder and a searing lightning flash, Silver Cloud returned.

He appeared on the lake shore, a small, misty figure in the far distance, growing larger as he galloped towards the mine. His hooves pounded the ground, splashed through water, kicked up spray. Sometimes he would vanish from Four Winds' vision, hidden by a flurry of rain and wind, or by a rock which came between them. And then the boy was afraid that he had imagined the horse and he would sink back under his ledge. 'This is another trick,' he would tell himself.

'A false hope to torture me.' Then he would curse Unktehi and stare into the distance to make doubly sure that his guardian dream horse wasn't there.

Silver Cloud sped through the rain and wind. He ignored the lightning, sent by Unktehi, which landed at his feet, and the blasts of thunder which cracked over his head. He had been away from Kola for more than a day and night, during which much had taken place. Now the boy took refuge from the storm at the entrance to the deepest mine. And he, Silver Cloud, was needed more than ever before.

The grey horse appeared again out of the rain. Four Winds saw that he was closer, more solid than before. His drenched mane was whipped back from his head, his neck stretched, his legs splashing and speeding towards the mine. Was this real, or was it another of Unktehi's cruel spirits in disguise? Still Four Winds would not allow himself to believe.

Braving the worst of the thunder and lightning, Silver Cloud reached the entrance to the mine. He shook his mane and endured the torrent, turning towards Kola and speaking as he had spoken before. 'I have returned.'

So Four Winds sprang from his shelter and raced towards the dream horse. He reached to touch Silver

Cloud's neck and run his hand down to his streaming shoulder.

'Believe it,' Silver Cloud assured him.

'But how?' Four Winds was almost unable to speak. He had seen the horse roped and tied, dragged away bleeding by Snake Eye and his band.

'Through the strength of Ghost Horse, messenger of Wakanda, I was delivered,' Silver Cloud replied. 'The Comanches hobbled me and thrust their spears into me. They left me lying dead on the earth.'

Four Winds gasped.

'They carry hate in their hearts. But Ghost Horse sees everything. He returned me to the Other World to meet with Wakanda and be healed by his power, which is greater than all others. Look, I have no wounds in my side!'

Four Winds saw that it was true. Silver Cloud was whole and strong. The boy's heart swelled with solemn wonder. 'My cousin, Hidden Moon, followed us,' he reported sadly. 'Unktehi's spirits killed her as she entered the mine.'

The horse nodded. 'Her name will live amongst the brave. And now we must honour her and complete the quest.'

Four Winds looked through the rain towards the

dark, overhanging entrance of the mine. Silver Cloud's words had stirred him and rekindled his courage. 'Without you to guide me I have made many mistakes,' he confessed.

'And you have also come far, and shown much courage,' the horse reminded him.

'You will stay now until we find the diamond?' Without Silver Cloud's calm presence, Kola doubted that he could succeed.

'I have sworn to stay by your side.'

The boy sighed. 'Then together we will defeat Unktehi as you have defeated Snake Eye,' he said in a low voice. 'First we must move the stones which crushed Hidden Moon.'

So they trudged through the storm to the cave which led into the mine and began to push aside rocks to clear the way. Rain still beat down from a leaden sky, slowing Four Winds down in his work of lifting and dragging the heavy debris.

As they worked, Kola looked over his shoulder at the dismal lake and the great canyon sides. He thought of Yietso and his huge, writhing coils of snake flesh, and of Unktehi, as yet invisible. A cold shudder ran through his body as he made himself lift the next stone and carry it with scraped and bleeding hands.

Silver Cloud sensed Kola's deep dread. He wished he had words to take away the fear and soothe the boy's grieving heart. But he knew that the answer lay beyond what he could say, deep in the mine beneath their feet.

At last, Kola rolled away the last rock which blocked the tunnel. He looked at Silver Cloud then stepped inside.

His footfall released a flash of lightning and a roar of thunder. They came at the same instant – the blinding light and the rumble – making Kola spin round and raise his arm to shield his eyes. He saw the dark outline of Silver Cloud framed in the entrance and beyond him, casting a great shadow, loomed the evil serpent shape of Yietso.

Fear came then and battered at Kola's heart. He saw the grinning jaws and the glaring emerald eyes, the shining black scales of the monster who had tricked him. And the taunting words came back, 'It is not yet time.'

Now though, Four Winds was closer than ever to discovering the diamond, and Silver Cloud was with him. So it seemed certain Yietso had returned in earnest.

Still, Silver Cloud didn't flinch as he stood between

the serpent monster and the boy. Even when the waves on the lake behind Yietso grew rough, as if troubled by a mighty wind, the horse faced the enemy without fear.

Holding his breath, Kola stole back towards the entrance. The waves on Yellow Water rose high up the sides of the canyon, hitting the rock with enormous force and casting spray back into the water. It was as if something underneath the surface was causing it – a mighty force heaving up towards the light from the dark depths.

A wave rushed up the near shore, tall as ten men. It crashed on the stony slope, over Hidden Moon's grave, then ran and leapt as white spray as far as the entrance to the mine. Silver Cloud felt it swirl around his legs.

Then the creature below the lake surfaced. It heaved itself into view, so huge that it took away Kola's breath. The horned giant spewed water from its mouth, rising on to two legs and surveying the canyon.

'Unktehi!' Silver Cloud breathed.

The monster rose slowly, letting the water run from its broad back. It was pale gold, the colour of the land around it, and its burning red eyes were set in dark sockets.

Four Winds crept alongside Silver Cloud.

'Don't be afraid. Unktehi cannot leave Yellow Water,'

the horse told the boy. 'In the lake no one can trouble him, for he is too powerful. But on land, Wakanda's force is stronger.'

'So why has he come?' Kola trembled at the sheer size of the water monster, who filled the base of the great canyon and whose eyes shone like red fires in the hissing storm.

'To talk with Yietso and guide him.' Silver Cloud watched the grinning serpent withdraw towards the shore. His black body writhed low on the ground, with only his flat head erect, until he reached the water.

'Then this is our chance!' Hurriedly Kola ran back to the mine, followed more slowly by the dream horse. 'Come!' he urged. 'What is the matter?'

'I hear horses galloping,' Silver Cloud replied, searching up and down the canyon.

'It is nothing but the rain!' Kola insisted. Their head start on Unktehi and Yietso must not be thrown away.

So he entered the mine a second time, only to find that his guide did not follow. 'Come!' he called again.

For a few moments Kola tried to find his own way down the rough, narrow tunnel. He touched the cold sides, felt the darkness close in on him and imagined the distance he must walk to find the diamond. Turning back towards the exit, he heard movement and expected to see the dream horse coming to join him.

But the figure he saw was that of a crouching man moving stealthily towards him. He trod soft as a mountain lion, holding a raised spear above his head.

And now Kola too heard the sound of galloping horses, and saw men and riders swarm around the entrance, led by a figure in a wolfskin headdress. Silver Cloud was quickly surrounded by whirling warriors on horseback.

This was Snake Eye and his band. They had followed footprints in the loose earth, ridden through the storm to find the Sioux boy. And now, amazed and angry that the spirit horse had returned, their war cries filled the air and they threatened to bring their raised tomahawks crashing down on Silver Cloud.

As Kola hesitated, so the warrior on foot crept nearer. In another flash which lit up the dark tunnel, Kola recognised the face of his hated enemy, Matotope.

The man who had betrayed his People paused and sneered at the boy's startled glance. 'Close your jaws and do not look so foolish. I am sworn brother now to Snake Eye. He is my Chief!'

No words formed on Kola's lips. There was a bitter

taste in his mouth as he stared into Matotope's narrow eyes.

'Stand aside!' Matotope ordered. 'I travelled ahead of my new brothers. It is my task to go into the deepest mine and bring back the diamonds for Snake Eye and the Comanches!'

'Never!' Kola stood firm. He took out his knife, given to him by Red Hawk. 'You must kill me first.'

Matotope laughed and made a stabbing gesture with his spear. He sprang towards Kola, who quickly stepped to one side. The lunge took the medicine man past him, into the darkness of the mine.

'I have Silver Cloud to guide me!' Kola warned. 'He has escaped you once. His power is strong.'

Once more Matotope cast aside the warning. Crouching again, the blade of his spear flashed and then he spoke. 'The power of Unktehi is stronger, and Snake Eye has called upon the master, Anteep, to guide him. Your dream horse will never defeat the might of the evil ones!'

Outside the tunnel, thunder crashed and horses' hooves clashed against the rock. Matotope's mocking words rang loud in Kola's ears.

But then, in a sudden flash from out of nowhere, Yietso was there. The black snake reared over

Matotope's head, his yellow throat glowing. The medicine man spun round, leaving his back unguarded.

Kola was poised, ready to plunge his knife between Matotope's bare shoulder blades. He saw the place where the blade should enter, to one side of the backbone, between the ribs.

Yietso's fierce gaze held back his arm and he couldn't strike. Then the monster turned his eyes towards Matotope. 'You dared to enter Unktehi's mine!' he challenged. 'What is your purpose here?'

'To kill the boy and prevent him from stealing the diamond.' Matotope's answer was cowed. He shrank back against the wall and let his spear drop to the ground.

Yietso swelled out his form until it blocked the way completely. 'This is a lie,' he hissed. 'I am everywhere in this mine. I know that you plan to cheat Unktehi and take the stone for yourself!'

'No! I swear to you that we are in the service of Anteep, leader of Unktehi. We would not steal the stone!'

'But I heard you confess your greed to the boy,' came the challenge. 'You cannot unsay what has already been said!'

'Then it was because Snake Eye ordered it!'

Matotope's voice grew high and soft as he twisted his way out of the blame. 'Believe me, I would not have undertaken the task if my life had not been in danger. The leader of my enemy, the Comanche Wild Dogs, made me do this!'

Yietso regarded him with a cold, cruel eye. 'You are not a newly sworn brother to Snake Eye, after all?'

A groan came from Matotope's throat. 'Yietso!' he pleaded. 'My heart is with you. Forget about the diamond. I will do anything you ask!'

The serpent monster lowered his head so that his flickering tongue played around Matotope's cheek. 'How is this? Betrayal is your nature,' he hissed.

'Believe me, I am your servant!' The medicine man fell to his knees.

' "Believe you"?' Yietso mocked. 'As Red Hawk, Chief of the White Water band, believed you when you ran from the battle at Thunder Ridge? As Snake Eye believed you when he sent you to fetch the diamond?'

'I came to do Snake Eye's work!' Matotope whined.

'No. You came for the stone. But your plan was to flee from Snake Eye once you had found it. There is no loyalty in you. You would betray all men!' Yietso delivered his judgement in a harsh voice, his face close to the man's.

'I give you my word!' Matotope cried.

The serpent drew coldly back. 'Your word is less than nothing,' he replied.

Saying this, he fixed his eyes on the guilty man, who felt the stare penetrate deep beneath his skin into his spirit. It ate into him like a bitter poison, hollowing out his body, leaving nothing but the shell.

Matotope rose in terror. As his body was eaten away from the inside and his heart stopped beating, he opened his mouth to speak.

'No more words!' Yietso commanded, increasing the intensity of his stare.

Kola saw that Matotope suffered great anguish, yet he could not understand why. The man seemed whole, but his mouth was twisted into a silent scream, and he clutched his chest, wildly beating his fist against his ribs. Only the gaze of the serpent held him in its power.

The beating of Matotope's fist grew weaker, he staggered and fell to his knees.

'Stop!' Kola pleaded with Yietso to end the traitor's pain.

But still the invisible poison ate away at Matotope. It seared him and made him raise his arms in silent plea.

There was nothing left of him, only bones that

wasted to dust even as he sank. Yet still his eyes saw the serpent. Until his last breath was taken, the man knew his tormentor and shrivelled under the glare of his green eyes.

EIGHT

Words had failed Matotope. The lies he had lived by were no more use. His life had ended in agonised silence.

Through his horror, Four Winds saw that this was fitting. But he was afraid for his own life now that Yietso had turned the medicine man to dust. So he fled from the mine, stumbling into the thunderstorm and the frantic whirlwind of horses and men.

The Wild Dogs had surrounded Silver Cloud and were racing their horses in an ever tightening circle.

Their spears were raised and their wild cries rose above the low, constant roll of thunder.

With Yietso behind him in the tunnel, the boy had no choice but to dart between the circling horses in an effort to reach his guardian. Risking his life, he lunged forward between two of the mounted Comanches, feeling the hot breath of their horses and the swipe of a tomahawk close to his skull.

'Kill him too!' Snake Eye snarled the command, wrenching the reins of his black-and-white horse to steer it out of the tight circle and ride to a nearby hill. Here he reined his mount to a standstill to look down on the destruction he had ordered.

Four Winds found Silver Cloud trapped in the centre of the warlike circle, still untouched by the weapons of the enemy. Time and again he reared on to his hind legs, striking out with his front hooves to ward off attack, but when he saw the boy he stopped for an instant to let him climb on to his back.

Gratefully Kola made the leap, then held tight to the silver horse's mane. He felt the strong body lunge forward as if to break through the circle, only to be driven back again by a jabbing spear. High on the hill, Snake Eye looked down with a dark frown.

Then Yietso the shape-shifter charged from the mine.

He had chosen the new form of a mighty black stallion, stronger than any horse ever seen, with wild eyes, flaring nostrils and ears pinned flat against his head.

The Comanche horses saw him and shied away.

'Hold the circle tight!' Snake Eye cried.

His band forced their horses to keep their positions while Yietso approached. When the black stallion veered to one side and charged through the rain down to the lake, they closed in on Silver Cloud and Kola once more.

Kola watched Yietso reach the shore and saw with renewed horror that Unktehi himself still squatted in the water, his vast bulk filling the canyon. As the two monsters met and planned their next move, he appealed to Silver Cloud. 'Must we die?' he whispered in terror.

His horse reared and struck out at the Comanches. 'We need powerful magic,' he replied. 'You must call quickly on the memory of your mother, Shining Star, while I turn day into night.'

With no time to question, Kola fulfilled the strange command. In the midst of the storm and the charging circle of enemy horses he closed his eyes and brought to mind his beautiful mother. She appeared with the soft look of love which he remembered, dark eyes melting as she gazed into his cradle, lips smiling, long dark hair falling loose over her shoulders.

As he remembered, so Silver Cloud called upon Ghost Horse to drive away the storm clouds. The powerful spirit brought a wind from the south which swept into the canyon and rolled the clouds over the northern ridge and dried up the rain. Ghost Horse made the sky dark, sending the sun behind the mountains to the west. Night fell, to the wild consternation of the Comanches and their horses.

'Day has become night!' they cried, letting their mounts shy away from the circle, making a space through which Silver Cloud could charge.

'The dream horse has defeated the Sun! Death has come to the day spirits of the sky!' The Wild Dogs broke away in fear.

Kola held tight as his horse charged through the weakening ring and set off at full gallop along the shore of the lake. He saw the moon appear as a pale crescent and the stars prick holes in the dark blanket of the night sky.

'Pursue them!' Quickly Snake Eye rallied his band. He led them in a race to capture Silver Cloud, leaning forward and urging his horse to cover the ground.

Meanwhile, Yietso had talked with Unktehi, whose dark presence still towered over the scene.

'Destroy the dream horse and the boy!' Unktehi passed a sentence of death. His red eyes glowed like giant coals through the black night. 'And do not let the Comanches live. They plotted with Matotope to steal the stone from deep in the mine. Though they swore allegiance to Anteep, they follow only their own desires!'

So Yietso kept the shape of the stallion and set off like a dark shadow in pursuit of all.

Hearing Comanche horses close on their heels, Kola glanced over his shoulder to see Snake Eye at their head. The chief's moonlit face was set in cruel lines beneath the wolfskin headdress. His spear glinted and a round, buffalo-skin shield swung loosely by his hip. Shouting the order for his band to fan out along the width of the shore, Snake Eye looked as though he would never give in.

'What now?' Kola breathed. Looking ahead, he saw that the giant canyon narrowed where the lake ended and that the plan of the Comanches was to overtake them and block their escape.

'Call once more upon Shining Star!' Silver Cloud told him. 'For though I can outrun Snake Eye, Yietso follows behind, and his power on land is stronger than mine.'

A second glance showed Kola the swift, strong shape of the black stallion drawing level with the Wild Dogs.

'In the air Yietso cannot touch us,' Silver Cloud promised. 'Call now upon your mother!'

Kola clung to Silver Cloud's mane and spoke to the night sky. 'Behold!' he cried. 'I am Four Winds, son of Swift Elk and Shining Star, from the band of the White Water Sioux! It is two summers since my father gave up his life for his People and my mother was taken by the Comanches. I call now upon Shining Star whose home is the night sky. Take us out of danger, into your arms!'

The time was right, and as he spoke, the silver stars in the heavens gathered together in a shining chain which lowered itself gently towards the earth. The chain spread its rays over Silver Cloud and his rider, enveloping them in a glow which separated them from their pursuers.

'Take hold of the end of the chain,' Silver Cloud told Kola, who reached up and touched the stars.

At that moment, the dream horse's hooves left the ground and rose slowly out of reach of Snake Eye. The Comanches looked on helplessly as the boy and the horse floated clear of the earth, high above their heads. Yietso too halted his swift stride and gazed in anger at the magical sight.

'Higher!' Four Winds begged the stars. He searched for his mother's face in the blackness overhead, but only heard her voice tenderly calling his name. 'Kola!' she sighed. 'My son!'

The chain of stars drew them higher. 'Mother!' Four Winds replied, his heart melting at the soft sounds.

'You have done well, my son!' she whispered.

Silver Cloud and Kola drifted into the sky, leaving behind their earthbound enemies.

Yietso turned then on Snake Eye. 'You are a fool!' he cried. 'You cannot destroy a mere boy of thirteen summers!'

'And you!' Snake Eye retorted. 'Your power is weak, in spite of your proud bearing.'

'A fool and a deceiver!' Yietso challenged, raising himself on to his hind legs. 'Yet your cunning wins you nothing except shame and defeat!'

The taunt drove Snake Eye into cruel action. Raising his spear, he chose his target and with deadly accuracy plunged the tip into the stallion's chest.

The Wild Dogs gasped and reined back their horses. As their chief drove his spear deep into Yietso's flesh, they saw the shape-shifter spill black blood. He fell to the earth and writhed, returning to the form of a serpent. From the lake, Unktehi roared out his anger.

Snake Eye jerked back his spear and drove his horse forward. Before Yietso could recover, he ran at him and trampled him, making him writhe and hiss.

Now the band of Comanches saw that the bitter actions of their leader had brought upon them a great trouble. They were full of dread and their cowardly hearts drove them away from the place where Snake Eye fought with Yietso. Reining their horses towards the end of the canyon, they set off in confusion, leaving Snake Eye to his fate.

Still Snake Eye attacked the monster, beating him down until he lay without movement, his blood spreading as a black pool under the horse's hooves.

Then at last the Comanche chief withdrew, raising his decorated spear into the air and yelling his defiance. 'I curse Yietso and his master, Unktehi! I will not follow Anteep! From this time Snake Eye will call upon no spirit to help him. For I am strong. Alone I will defeat my enemies!'

His voice echoed down the canyon and into the night sky where Silver Cloud and Four Winds were held by a swaying thread of stars. 'I am strong. Alone I will defeat my enemies!'

Snake Eye wheeled his horse around to follow his

fleeing band. Rearing him up, he shook his spear one last time. Then he galloped away, the hand of revenge gripped tight around his heart.

Four Winds heard the proud, bitter message. He looked to the heavens to hear Shining Star's tender voice soothe away his fear, but though he listened hard, he met with disappointment. There was silence over his head as the night sky faded into dawn and the gentle stars lowered him slowly back to earth.

NINE

'Two have died,' Silver Cloud warned. He stood with Kola before the dark entrance to the mine.

The boy already knew the danger of entering. With his own hands, he had lifted the stones from Hidden Moon's body. He had seen Matotope fade into dust.

'I have the plaited bracelet which my cousin made,' he told Silver Cloud. 'And the lizard skin pouch with the sacred cord. Lizard means long life,' he said with a brave smile.

'You will have need of good omens and the gifts

213

of your grandfather, Red Hawk.' Silver Cloud watched Kola open his medicine bundle and lay out the objects at the entrance to the tunnel.

Once more the boy chose the feather necklace for speed and this time a knot of sweetgrass to purify his cause. He rubbed the grass against the skin of his face and arms, saying, 'Behold me. The diamond we seek is sacred. May our enemies sleep, may the journey end in reward, for our quest is just!'

Then he rolled up the bundle and slung it across his shoulder. 'Snake Eye has smitten Yietso with his spear. At least we have one less enemy to fear.'

But his wise guardian shook his head. 'As with me, so it is with Yietso. He will return to Anteep, head of the underworld, to be renewed. A ceremony will make him whole again.'

'Then we must begin our journey into the mine before he returns,' Kola said, clenching his fists in an effort to master his fear.

'Unktehi has many other spirits who guard the diamonds,' Silver Cloud said, looking intently along the length of the lake. Daylight had returned, together with brooding clouds which had settled along the high ridge marking the edge of the canyon. At the death of Yietso, Unktehi had withdrawn below the surface of the lake, no doubt to make another plan aimed at defeating the intruders.

Following the horse's gaze, Kola couldn't pick out any sign of danger. Yet he knew that the smallest creature could present a hidden threat, even the spider who wove her webs in cracks in the rock.

'We will not succeed by the knife and spear,' Silver Cloud predicted. 'Unktehi will send spirits too strong and cruel for us to overcome. So it is as I said in the beginning: sometimes battle is not the way.'

'What then?' Kola was ready to give all his boy's strength to the fight, and eager now to begin.

'We must be wiser than our enemy, and trick him. Unktehi watches us from his underwater lair. As soon as we enter the mine, he will set his monsters upon us to draw us back.'

Kola felt his skin crawl at the notion of Unktehi's red gaze fixed upon them. 'How do we prevent them?' he asked.

Silver Cloud walked slowly under the dark overhang and peered inside. His silver grey coat made him look ghostly, his noble head was raised, his ears pricked and listening. 'We will take a risk,' he decided, casting his gaze towards the rocks strewn down the slope. 'We will let Unktehi see us enter and send his spirits after us. But before they reach us, I will bring down another great fall of rock.'

The danger was so great that it took away Kola's breath. 'You will block the tunnel?' he gasped.

'Yes, and make Unktehi believe that we died like Hidden Moon, crushed under the collapsing tunnel.'

'But we will stay ahead of the rockfall!' Though the risk was great, the plan was clever. 'Then we can go deep into the mine without Unktehi's spirits giving chase. But when we return to the rockfall, what then? Won't our way be blocked and all our efforts wasted?'

Silver Cloud turned kindly towards the boy. 'When you hold the diamond in your hand, then our journey is ended,' he explained. 'Ghost Horse will return us to Red Hawk and your People faster than the lightning strikes the earth.'

With this hope in his heart and complete trust in the dream horse, Four Winds accepted the plan. They entered the mine together, under Unktehi's jealous gaze.

The water monster summoned Washoe, the great bird of Lake Tahoe in the south west, and the white water buffaloes from Bull Lake to the west. Then he called upon the myriad of water babies from Yellow Water itself, small people with long hair that swept down from their heads and cloaked their bodies, whose task was to guard the hot springs. He called from the mountains a great giant with one eye which glowed in his forehead, called Numuzo'ho, the Crusher of Men. Lastly, he gathered his many serpents, lizards, frogs, owls and eagles. But he did not call on anyone who might break through rock.

'Follow the horse and the boy,' Unktehi told his servants. 'The horse is messenger to Ghost Horse and has many powers. Crush them both!'

So Washoe the giant bird flapped his heavy wings and took flight towards the mine, ahead of the buffaloes and the water babies who clung to the thick hair around their necks. Numuzo'ho, with his glowing eye, strode after them, ready to destroy.

Kola stepped into the darkness with Silver Cloud at his side. They heard the rush of a giant bird's wings beating the air and the thunderous steps of their many pursuers.

'Make ready!' Silver Cloud urged Kola forward. 'Take ten steps and then wait.'

With his heart thumping hard against his ribs and his mouth dry with terror, he obeyed the command.

Five paces into the blackness, he paused and turned. Behind him was the square of daylight and his connection with the world he knew. Ahead was the dark unknown.

'Walk further!' Silver Cloud commanded.

Still Kola hesitated. He pictured the rocks falling from the roof, cutting out the light. What if the way ahead was also blocked? He would be imprisoned in stone and breathe his last breath in darkness. Every instinct cried out against it.

But he loved the horse and trusted him with his life. 'I will never fail you. Love sits in my heart,' Silver Cloud had promised at Talking Gods Rock. This then was the greatest test.

So, with trembling legs, Kola did his bidding, feeling the darkness throw its damp cloak around him, following in the footsteps of poor Hidden Moon.

From the lake, Unktehi watched his horde of evil spirits surge towards the mine. Washoe alighted on the rocky ledge above the entrance, sending in the small water babies, who scuttled into the darkness, their long hair streaming behind.

Silver Cloud saw the creatures enter. Summoning all his power, he forced the rock above his head to crack. It split with a grinding shudder, sending a fault line shooting along the roof of the tunnel towards Unktehi's followers.

Fatally weakened, the roof straight away started to crumble on to the water babies, piling rock upon rock so that soon Kola could only see a narrow gap through which daylight entered. He put his hands to his ears to dull the crack and thud of falling rock. 'Silver Cloud!' he called out, as the last rays of light disappeared.

All was dark and quiet. The last rock had wedged itself into the final gap. The wall was complete. Kola could hear his own breath. 'Silver Cloud!' he cried again.

A silver white glimmer appeared at his side. 'It is done,' the horse said.

Unktehi rose from the lake in anger once more. He raged at Washoe and Numuzo'ho. 'Clear a path!' he roared.

'But the horse and the boy are dead,' Washoe protested. He'd heard the howls of the water babies and pictured the scene of destruction inside the tunnel.

'How can you be sure?' Unktehi needed proof. 'Dig through the rockfall!' he commanded Numuzo'ho. 'Bring me their crushed and lifeless bodies!'

As the giant began to heave at the rocks, Silver Cloud and Kola set off on the last stage of their journey.

Instead of pitch blackness, the silver glow from the horse's body cast a pale light – enough to show the uneven ground underfoot and the twists and bends in the sloping tunnel.

'It is as if the earth has swallowed us!' Kola whispered, picturing the weight of rock above their heads. He kept his hand on Silver Cloud's neck and took his pace from him.

'Yet men tore out this rock and dug this mine,' the horse reminded him. 'Many exhausted slaves lost their lives in the search for the glittering stone.'

Kola examined the rough marks on the rock walls. It was true: the tunnel had been gouged out with flint blades, step by step. The path to the diamond was stained with dead men's blood. But he did not have time to wonder, as every step took them closer to the end of their first journey.

Soon the sloping ground gave way to steep steps cut into the rock, taking them deeper. Water began to trickle through the roof and form narrow streams, falling as small waterfalls down the worn steps. They ran into a pool in an underground cavern which widened out before Silver Cloud and Kola.

The boy shook his head in wonder. He had not known that the rock beneath his feet contained streams and caves, nor that the stone could form strange icicles which hung the height of a man from the roofs. His feet splashed through shallow pools as he held firmly to Silver Cloud's mane.

'The trick of the rockfall worked well.' Kola's voice echoed through the eerie cavern. He could hear no footsteps behind them and his fear began to ease.

'Unless Unktehi suspects and orders his giants to remove the stones.' Silver Cloud knew his enemy well. But he realised that the trick had given them more time.

They passed through the high cavern, back into a tunnel, and followed more steps deeper into the earth.

Kola wondered how far they must continue. He stumbled in his eagerness.

'Do not fall now!' Silver Cloud warned.

Down they went. The tunnel grew narrower, so that Silver Cloud had to lower his head. His sides swayed against the walls, his hooves clattering on the uneven stone.

'Dig faster!' Unktehi told Numuzo'ho. He grew certain that the horse and the boy were not dead after all.

The giant clawed at boulders and tore rocks from the entrance to the mine, which the buffalo spirits rolled down the hill into the lake. Washoe circled overhead, swooping to pick up rocks between his great claws and let them drop into the water. The bird saw black clouds gather on the ridge and welcomed them as signs of ill omen. He circled higher and cried out a message to Unktehi below. 'Behold, Yietso is here!'

The guardian of the mine looked up and saw the black serpent appear at the edge of the canyon. The ritual to renew him in the World Beneath had been speedy; he had returned life-side to help defeat Silver Cloud and the boy.

'Let me enter the mine!' he hissed at Unktehi, seeing that Numuzo'ho had opened up a narrow gap into the tunnel. 'For I am the power that can defeat the enemy!'

Unktehi gave his assent. 'Go quickly!' he commanded. 'For the boy grows close to the diamond!'

Deep under the earth, Kola crouched as the tunnel narrowed.

'I cannot go on!' Silver Cloud told him. 'You must continue alone!'

So the boy stooped and edged forward, hoping that the way ahead was not long and that he would soon reach the bottom of the mine. There was rock all around him, no sky or sun. Only the darkness leading to the diamond.

He went on to his hands and knees, feeling his way. Cold water trickled on to him and the rough stone scraped his skin. And then at last he reached the end.

It was a small chamber lit by a dull green light. Kola found that he could stand, and looked around, wondering about the source of the light.

On a ledge there was a buffalo-skin bundle bound with thongs, much like the medicine bundle he carried across his shoulder. The boy's heart leapt when he saw it. He ran towards it.

But a shadow hovered by the ledge, resting on a rock, coiled and dangerous. A snake raised its head, its emerald eyes glowing.

Yietso! Kola's hand had almost touched the bundle on the ledge before he saw the serpent and recoiled.

The snake's tongue flickered, ready to strike.

The boy's hand went towards his knife. Yietso would not stand between him and his prize! He would fight the evil spirit with all his might.

The serpent hissed and writhed towards him.

Drawing his grandfather's blade, and calling out the name of Red Hawk in a clear voice, Kola felt no fear. This blade would strike like lightning. It would overcome the worst of enemies.

And yet he had never struck in anger in all his thirteen summers. He felt his hand tremble as the snake began to wind its body around him. Then he thought of all that had passed on this journey, and the prize that was still to be won. So he brought the knife up in the name of his father and all who had been slain by the Comanches, and in the name of all his People who were to be saved.

The blade slashed against Yietso's soft throat. But it was not the force of the knife in his flesh that paralysed the creature and made him slide to the ground. It was the power of Swift Elk, who was treacherouly slain, and the strength of the White Water People, whose spirits were greater than the evil of Yietso and his lord, Unktehi.

Kola withdrew his knife and watched the serpent sink lifeless to the ground.

He turned to seize the bundle from the ledge, then ran from the chamber, scrambling through the tunnel to rejoin Silver Cloud. He held up the leather parcel, untying it with trembling fingers, using his knife when his fingers proved too weak.

The dream horse stood by silently and watched.

At last Kola opened the tightly wrapped bundle. He

spread it on the ground in the pale silver light, turned it this way and that until he realised that it was empty.

'No!' he gasped, and searched again.

There were no glittering stones.

Four Winds looked up at Silver Cloud in dismay. He felt a tight band of sorrow around his chest. The picture of his grandfather, Red Hawk, and his grandmother, White Deer, wringing their hands in despair, struck him to the heart. And he thought of brave Hidden Moon.

The boy slumped bitterly to the ground. '*Hena 'la yelo.*' It is over.

As he bowed forward in defeat, tears welled from deep within. They rose through his wounded heart, washing it clean. And they appeared in his brown eyes, shining in the light.

Silver Cloud watched and waited.

Kola's tears brimmed over and fell on to the empty bundle. They turned into bright, glittering diamonds – the purest and most perfect ever seen.

The boy reached out and took up one of the glittering stones. As his finger closed around the diamond, he smiled at the dream horse through his tears.

Then Four Winds and Silver Cloud called upon Ghost Horse, and the spirit took them home.

THE RETURN

'I will speak again,' Red Hawk said. He held up the diamond from the deepest mine for his People to see.

Four Winds stood by his side.

'The son of my only son, Swift Elk, has made his journey with the dream horse. They have sought out the first prize of three and suffered much to bring it home.'

White Deer's face ran with tears of pride. 'Praise the goodness of the Great Spirit, Wakanda,' she murmured. 'That he has brought my grandson safely back to my arms.'

Red Hawk's gnarled fingers closed around the precious stone. 'Now there is a gleam of light in the east for the White Water band. Though frost whitens the trees and ice freezes the streams, there is hope that we may yet overcome Snake Eye and his Wild Dogs.'

Four Winds heard the sigh of satisfaction that passed between the warriors, the women and the children. It was like wind amongst pale aspen leaves.

'We have lost our brave child, Hidden Moon,' Red Hawk went on. His old eyes searched the evening sky for the first pale glint of stars in the heavens. 'She is with Wakanda, where the noble spirits of our fathers rest.'

The People murmured their praise of a girl who had given her life for their future.

In Kola's mind's eye, her brown eyes flashed. Her voice said, as if from a great distance, 'I will go with you to find the precious stone!' When they were children, playing by the tipi, he had taught her to pull a taut bowstring and aim true. Now Thunder Bird stood guard over her grave.

Tomorrow, at dawn, as he stepped out of the village with Silver Cloud on his second journey to find the feather from the highest mountain, he would carry the memory of Hidden Moon with him.

Gravely his grandfather took an eagle's feather from his own war bonnet and gave it to Four Winds. '*Iki 'cize waon 'kon,*' he said softly. 'Once I was a warrior. Now it is the turn of the young and swift.'

The boy took the feather and ran his thumb along the soft, silken edge. Then he tied this badge of honour to the leather thong which bound his precious medicine bundle.

He looked up and met the dream horse's wise gaze. *Now I am a warrior too.*

If you enjoyed Silver Cloud - look out for book two in the Dreamseeker trilogy - coming soon...

Jenny Oldfield

IRON EYES

Four Winds must leave his grandfather and his tribe and fulfil three seemingly impossible tasks: to fetch a diamond from the deepest mine, a feather from the highest mountain, and a breath of wind from the furthest ocean. Only then will his tribe be spared.

The quest continues...

Hodder Children's Books

If you enjoyed Silver Cloud - look out for book three in the Dreamseeker trilogy - coming soon...

Jenny Oldfield's

BAD HEART

Four Winds must leave his grandfather and his tribe and fulfil three seemingly impossible tasks: to fetch a diamond from the deepest mine, a feather from the highest mountain, and a breath of wind from the furthest ocean. Only then will his tribe be spared.

The quest continues...